Emajen

First published by Our Street Books, 2018
Our Street Books is an imprint of John Hunt Publishing Ltd., Laurel House, Station Approach,
Alresford, Hants, SO24 9JH, UK
office1@jhpbooks.net
www.johnhuntpublishing.com
www.ourstreet-books.com

For distributor details and how to order please visit the 'Ordering' section on our website.

Design: Stuart Davies

Printed and bound by CPI Group (UK) Ltd, Croydon, CR0 4YY, UK

We operate a distinctive and ethical publishing philosophy in
all areas of our business, from our global network of authors to
production and worldwide distribution.

Emajen

Ashley Ledigo

**OUR STREET
BOOKS**

Winchester, UK
Washington, USA

For Tony: Muse, inspiration, soul mate. Thank you for always being there.

For Emma: the greatest gift life could bestow.

And for Shadow: much missed and hopefully grazing peacefully somewhere...

CHAPTER ONE

Lightning slashed across the storm-swept sky. Crevitos towered, deliberately menacing, as his dark cloak whipped around him, bullied by the brutish wind. The violent electric storm seemed only to heighten Crevitos's cruel beauty; he stood, tall and imposing, casting tendrils of fear into the hearts and minds of every creature cowered there before him.

'Now!' he cried raising his fists in triumph. 'Now, bow to me. Scrape, you vermin, crawl. I am master and henceforth this place has a new name: *"Doomland"*, because you are all DOOMED!' His speech concluded with a screaming cackle. Groups of creatures of varied shapes, sizes and colours, huddled together. They were alike only in their misery.

Crevitos lowered his gaze, his large piercing eyes seeming to fasten on each one of them. They felt his glare burn through their souls like acid. Seeing their abject misery, his mouth curled sadistically: a parody of a smile. Even in their wretchedness they wondered how such cruelty, such loathsome evil could emanate from such impressive beauty. Lowering his voice to a threatening snarl, he bent forward to impress his next point with fierce clarity.

'Don't think,' he hissed, 'even for a nanosecond, about disobeying my orders. Everything...EVERYTHING, is punishable by *death*!' The last word was whispered so quietly that it might easily have been whipped away, unheard, by the howling wind. But it was so menacing that not one of the creatures shivering wretchedly below could possibly have missed its import.

* * *

'So whadya think?' Martin creased his forehead expectantly.

'Yeah, gruesome!' Tom handed the comic strip reverently

1

back to his friend. 'You've always been good at this stuff.'

'Drawing cartoons is all I've ever wanted to do. Anyway, the paper seemed to like it.'

'Does that mean they've offered you the job?'

'Well more or less, I mean, because I'm only seventeen, I've really got to start at the bottom doing basic stuff, you know? I won't be drawing my own cartoons yet.'

Tom lounged back in his chair, lacing long tapered pianist's fingers behind his head. Their talents had drawn them together: the artist and the musician, neither one quite fitting the teenage mould. Tom had been there at Crevitos's creation. He had watched as Crevitos blossomed into the violent, sadistic, ruthless leader of 'Doodleland' – that place where every creation drawn by man took shape and came to life.

'I like the change of name,' he said, ' "Doomland", it's creepy. So what happens to Crevitos now?'

Martin shrugged. He had other things on his mind. 'Oh, I think it's time I gave Crevitos a rest. He's kind of old hat anyway.'

* * *

Crevitos breathed in hugely. A wall of silence, like death, hung over the dark fortress he called home. Not a sound could escape those immense, forbidding stone walls. In his dark eyrie, hundreds of feet up in the sky, a single lamp shone, doing nothing to disperse the oppressive shadows. He liked it this way. From here he could survey Doomland and revel in the barren waste it had become. He felt a surge of power sweep through him. Energy pulsated around him with a visible iridescent glow that radiated pure evil. Finally he let out a roar of triumph. 'Free at last! No longer the slave to a mere boy's whim. World beware!'

CHAPTER TWO

Pat, pat. Curl. Bump. Wide green eyes stared unblinkingly for a moment in mock surprise. The tiny, green, fuzzy object pinged. A paw shot out as quickly as lightning. Destiny giggled. 'Oh, Torny, you're so funny!'

The kitten looked at her enquiringly, stuck his tongue out and promptly somersaulted over the rung of the chair. Destiny laughed again. Then she sighed, as she turned her thoughts toward her English homework. She wished it were maths. Maths was easy, in fact she could calculate stuff in her head that other kids needed calculators for. She rubbed her eyes and tried to read the page again.

Mum came in. She looked at Destiny's scowl of concentration and a frown creased her own forehead.

'Destiny?'

Destiny looked up and made a rueful face at her mum.

'Are you struggling with that, babe? Come on, I'll give you a hand.'

'If you could just read it for me, Mum, that would help. I can answer the questions, it's just, well, the letters seem to dance around and the harder I try, the more confused I get.'

Destiny's mum raised her eyebrows, but said nothing. She sat down to read the passage.

* * *

'Sounds like she could be dyslexic to me.'

Jenny Smith looked concerned. Dyslexia wasn't something she knew much about.

'I thought it was more a boy thing,' she told her friend.

'Well, tends to be, but not exclusively. How long has she been seeing dancing letters?'

'I'm ashamed to say, I don't really know.' Jenny shook her head. 'She only told me a few days ago. But I don't understand it, I mean she gets such good grades in maths and…you've seen her drawings. She seems such a bright kid.'

'Dyslexia has nothing to do with intelligence,' Becky retorted, somewhat tersely. 'I seem to remember someone telling me once that Einstein was dyslexic!' At Jenny's expression, Becky immediately felt sorry for her brusqueness. 'It's okay,' she said, more gently, 'I know just the guy to help you.'

* * *

Destiny read through the page that Mr Porter had given her, reasonably fluently. She stumbled a bit, but felt that she had done okay. Some of the other tests were not so good. She kept writing her Bs and Ds the wrong way round and couldn't make up her mind between several versions of the same spelling. Some of the tests were plain weird. She had to stand on one leg with her eyes closed for ten seconds. She wobbled disastrously after three and collapsed after five. She felt a totally inappropriate urge to giggle and was astounded when Mr Porter let out a throaty chuckle.

'I have trouble with that one too. Now,' he asked, 'tell me about these dancing letters. Mum says they're getting to be a bit of a problem.'

Destiny laughed. It was a relief. She liked Mr Porter. 'Well,' she considered, 'it doesn't happen all the time. But sometimes it's like there are two of every letter overlapping and then they sort of move up and down. Then I get really confused.'

'Does this happen more when you're tired?'

Destiny looked surprised, 'I guess…yeah, I think it does.'

Up to this point, Jenny had forced herself not to interrupt or interfere. Now she said miserably, 'I just don't understand, you've read whole books; how did you do that?'

Destiny was surprised by her mother's outburst. She shrugged her shoulders.

'I don't know,' she replied unhappily.

Mr Porter intervened quietly, 'Do you find that you guess a lot of the time, especially once you know what the subject is about?'

'That's exactly it,' said Destiny excitedly. 'It's like stories are easy because a lot of the time you kind of know what's going to happen.' Then her face fell. 'But now I'm in secondary school, Mum, some of the stuff we have to read is really hard.'

'But you're in top set for English, so you must be doing something right.'

'I think you'll find, that for someone as clever as Destiny, it's actually quite easy to bluff your way through primary English!' Mr Porter smiled at Destiny and she thought she detected just the merest hint of a wink.

She looked relieved. 'So I'm not stupid then?'

'Far from it, my dear, and there is a great deal that can be done to help this particular problem.'

'So in your opinion, she is dyslexic then?' Jenny interrupted again.

'If you must give it a label, yes.' Mr Porter scratched his head absentmindedly. 'However, we'll only use a label in so far as it can be used to your –' he looked at Destiny – 'advantage for exams and things.'

'Oh cool!' Destiny looked much happier.

'Now, recent theories are much more based on improving balance and hand to eye co-ordination, so I'm going to ask you to work on a series of exercises…'

CHAPTER THREE

'All set? We've got to go!' Mum said firmly.

Destiny pouted behind her mum's back. This was not a trip she was looking forward to – two weeks on a ranch in America, riding into the sunset every wretched day. Mum had always been mad about riding. Destiny loved horses – she loved all animals – but the idea of bouncing uncomfortably around on one and most likely ending up in a pile of something smelly, really didn't appeal. And for *two* weeks!

'Destiny, come ON!'

With a sigh of resignation, Destiny gave Tornado and Quaver one more affectionate kiss on the head each.

'Don't worry,' she whispered, 'Josh will look after you really well.' Josh was the boy next door, who looked after the two cats whenever Destiny and her mum went away, not to mention the two fish and the tortoise. Destiny was passionate about her animals and Josh was the only person she really trusted to look after them. He was good with them and spent time with the cats in case they were lonely.

'I'm not going to tell you again!' Mum sounded seriously like she was losing her rag.

'I'm coming,' Destiny shouted hurriedly. She heaved her suitcase up with both hands and waddled out to the waiting taxi.

Although the thought of flying was exciting Destiny beyond measure, she wasn't about to let her mum off the hook too lightly. She still couldn't believe that her mum had booked up a whole two weeks riding holiday, without checking first that it was actually something Destiny wanted to do. America. Great. Sandy beaches, luxurious accommodation, sunning by a sumptuous pool. Maybe even Disneyland Florida! But *nooo*. Mum had to book up a holiday on some crummy ranch somewhere in the middle of nowhere. The rationale being (Mum

6

was always careful to explain her rationale) that riding would help to improve Destiny's balance and would therefore fit in perfectly with her current dyslexia regime. Sure, there *was* a pool but, apart from that, if you didn't want to be with horses twenty-four seven, what else was there to do?

Destiny's mum broke into her train of thought.

'Come on miss smile-a-minute, we have to go to the departure lounge.'

Destiny couldn't keep up the pretence any more. Her natural enthusiasm spilled over and she grinned at her mum.

The first and longest part of the journey was from London to Las Vegas. What Destiny found peculiar, was that the flight took ten hours and forty-five minutes and yet, because of the time difference, they actually arrived in Las Vegas only two hours and forty-five minutes after they'd left London. It was odd to get your head around!

Everything on the plane fascinated Destiny, from the dinky little food trays to the individual TVs in the backs of the chairs. As the plane rose smoothly from the tarmac, she clutched her mum's hand and squeezed her eyes shut, waiting for her stomach to find a resting place a little farther south than her throat. The time passed surprisingly quickly. By the time she'd had a meal, read a bit and watched a film, the pilot was saying that they would soon be landing and giving them various snippets of information about the time, temperature and weather. Destiny sucked her boiled sweet hard, as the plane began its descent. She couldn't quite help a squeak of apprehension, as the plane bumped down onto the runway. She heard someone behind them remark what a smooth landing it was and wondered, in that case, what a bumpy one would be like. She decided she didn't want to know.

A waft of suffocating air hit them as they stepped from the air-conditioned interior of the aeroplane out into the scorching sunshine. Destiny couldn't believe how hot it was.

'It's set to get hotter,' chirruped her mum cheerily. 'I checked it on the internet before we left.'

'Mum, I'm a walking sweat-band as it is!' But Destiny couldn't help a skip as she walked. Maybe this holiday wasn't going to be so bad after all.

After a short stop, they had a couple of hours flight to Salt Lake City, followed by another short stop and the final one hour flight to Jackson Hole. By the time they had completed the journey and battled their way through customs, it was late, so Destiny's mum had booked them into a hotel for the night.

They both slept well and the huge range of choices on the breakfast menu made Destiny giggle. The journey from the hotel to the ranch did nothing to dampen Destiny's enthusiasm. For a start, someone had told the tour guide (and Mum swore it wasn't her) that Destiny would be twelve during their stay. He made everyone on the coach sing happy birthday to her, which was embarrassing (but rather nice) and presented her with a bouquet of flowers.

Most of the other passengers alighted at one of the two other places that the coach stopped at. Destiny looked on with awe. They were actually on the outskirts of a town. She could see tennis courts and the shimmer of water not too far away. Things really did look quite promising. It wasn't until the last people had disembarked from the coach and she and her mother were the only ones left on board, that the doubts began to creep back in. The tour guide chatted animatedly to Jenny as Destiny gazed more and more morosely out of the window. All signs of civilization soon fizzled out and there was no hint of tourist activity, or anything that seemed to suggest any kind of holiday resort.

At last the coach turned up a dirt track, which seemed to wind on interminably. Through the coach window, Destiny watched the spiky, purple-berried trees go by. They were beautiful in a sinister kind of way that matched her slightly darkening mood.

As they drove round a bend in the trees, the track suddenly widened into a huge, curving paved drive. Destiny sucked her breath in sharply. The house in front of her – well, mansion it would appear – stood proud and majestic, almost flaunting its white vastness as it shimmered through the heat haze.

CHAPTER FOUR

'Oh, WOW! This is it?'

The guide beamed and placed a rather battered looking leather hat on his head.

'Welcome –' he gestured widely – 'to Grey Ranch!'

The house was so impressive that Destiny felt a thrill of excitement running through her. 'I bet they've got a gigantic swimming pool and dancing and table tennis – oooh.' She squirmed with anticipation and followed her mum out of the coach.

She glanced around, trying to feel the atmosphere of the place, while her mum chatted nineteen-to-the-dozen with a cheery, grey-haired man who was balancing their luggage on a trolley.

'Hey, Mum—' Destiny was cut short by the most horrendous noise she had ever heard. It was a cross between a scream and a howl. Without thinking, Destiny flung aside her hand luggage and sprinted frantically in the direction of the noise.

Two men were standing just feet away from a dog. One of the men was desperately trying to grab hold of the dog by its collar.

Teeth gnashed, dripping saliva. The dog yowled again.

Destiny was about to launch herself at the man (what the hell was he doing?) when she realized what had happened.

The dog had caught its paw in a loose strand of wire attached to the fence. In its desperate efforts to escape the pain, it had pulled the wire taut until it was cutting the soft flesh with unremitting intensity. The dog thrashed and screamed. It lunged at the man, unaware that he was trying to help and yelped again as the wire bit once more into its now slippery, scarlet paw.

Destiny's mind flipped into overdrive.

'Stand on the wire!' she screamed.

The men spun round in astonishment. With a flash of understanding, the man who was standing watching rushed forward, planting a sturdy boot firmly on the wire.

'Wire cutters.' Destiny gasped. The other man sprang into action. Destiny approached the dog slowly.

'Hey, young lady, don't...'

But Destiny was in a world of her own. She stared hard at the dog until she caught its eye. Then she licked her lips, sighed and turned her head away. The second man returned with the clippers and cut the wire, which immediately loosened its vicious hold on the dog's paw. He turned to comfort the dog, which was whimpering now, but it snarled and cowered, shaking.

'Hey, Harriet, hey, girl, it's okay,' he half soothed, half pleaded.

Destiny ignored him. She kept fixing her gaze on the dog, then sighing, licking her lips and looking away. When she was only a foot or so away, she squatted down, talking in a low, soft voice, careful now not to look the dog straight in the eye.

'Harriet,' she crooned over and over, 'is that your name? Good girl. Good baby'

The dog visibly began to relax. The shaking gradually subsided. Still Destiny didn't make any attempt to touch her. Around them, in the yard, there was not a noise to be heard. The whole ranch seemed to hold its breath.

Unaware of anything but Harriet, Destiny waited patiently, not moving, just crooning gently. At last Harriet gave a little whimper and licked her lips. Finally, she stretched out her neck to sniff at Destiny. She licked the girl's hand. Slowly, calmly, Destiny stroked Harriet's head, talking soothingly all the time. Within a few minutes Harriet had buried her nose under Destiny's arm and was allowing her to look at the damaged paw.

When Destiny finally looked up, she had a smile on her face.

'No permanent damage, I don't think, but you'd better get the vet just in case.'

'I sure don't know how you did that, ma'am, but thank you all the same!' The man who had run to fetch the wire cutters held out his hand.

'Dan,' he said, by way of introduction.

'Destiny.' The reply was somewhat squeaky as her hand was crushed in a grip of iron.

'DESTINY!'

'Oh, oh, I'm in trouble!' Destiny's smile faded. Jenny came striding across the ground with long, angry steps.

'What the hell...'

Sensing a threat to her newfound friend, Harriet sprang to Destiny's defence, planting herself firmly between the girl and her aggressor. Lips quivered with menacing warning and a low growl rippled between them. Jenny stopped in her tracks. A look of astonishment replacing the angry concern.

It was one of those moments that seemed to stretch like an elastic band into a void where you could almost hear a pin drop...

It was broken by a throaty chuckle as Dan slapped his thigh.

'Sure ain't nothing wrong with that paw!'

The elastic band snapped.

Everyone began to laugh!

As Destiny and her mother walked to the cabin that was to be theirs for a fortnight, Jenny made a half-hearted attempt to berate her daughter.

'You know you could have been really hurt!'

Destiny muttered, 'Sorry,' in what she hoped was a shame-faced voice, but she couldn't help noticing a certain pride in her mother's complaint.

'I really didn't think. I just saw a dog in pain, that's all!' She half expected her mother to say, 'You never *do* think, that's the problem,' which was her usual response. However, Jenny just grunted which Destiny, somewhat relieved, took to mean that the scolding was over.

The cabin turned out to be more like a mini ranch house.

It smelt of wood and Destiny immediately relaxed and felt at home. All mod cons were supplied, including satellite TV.

'I bet that'll never even get turned on!' challenged Jenny.

'Bet it will!' But Destiny was too busy leaping the stairs two at a time to make the point by turning it on straight away. In her bedroom the bed was huge and soft, though not saggy. She crossed to the window and was staggered by the view.

'Bet there's nothing else to do once you've looked at that a hundred times,' she muttered, belatedly remembering that she was supposed to be cross about the whole holiday.

As she descended the stairs, there was a knock at the door. A boy about Destiny's age put his head through the opening and grinned. Destiny decided it was a nice face: cheeky, dimpled smile under blue eyes and unruly blond hair.

'Dad says if you come on up to the house there'll be a welcome drink...and a thank you one.' He grinned at Destiny.

'You go ahead, sweetheart,' said Jenny rather too brightly. 'I'll follow in a minute...just got to finish this case.'

'Muuum.' Destiny's tone was alarmed. Her expression clearly stated that her mum couldn't possibly be expecting her to go off, on her own, with a strange boy she'd only met for two minutes.

However, Jenny's raised eyebrows and puckered mouth suggested that it was one of those 'non-negotiable' things that cropped up from time to time.

The boy – Anthony, as Destiny discovered he was called – chattered amiably, telling her about the stables and the horses.

'I'll show you round later, if you like.'

'Oh, thanks!' Destiny realized she hadn't really been listening, but she discovered that she felt completely at ease with Anthony. She also noticed something else.

'You know it's weird,' she mused, 'you don't really have an American accent.'

Anthony's brow clouded for a moment.

'It's a long story,' he said gruffly. Then he grinned. 'I think your mum has decided to play chaperone after all!'

Destiny glanced behind. Sure enough, there was Mum hurrying along about two hundred yards back.

'Wow! You've got good hearing!' She was impressed.

'Mum always said I could hear a pin drop a mile off.'

Destiny noticed his use of the past tense, but decided now was not the time to be nosy. Instead she turned around and smiled at her mum who, slightly breathless, had caught up with them at last.

The gathering was very pleasant. Anthony's dad introduced them to the people who worked there and to a handful of other guests who were also staying there. There were no other children and it suddenly occurred to Destiny that Anthony must be very lonely. It was also fairly obvious that there was no Mrs Grey on the scene, although Mr Grey introduced them to his sister whom, he said, was the best cook this side of the Rockies.

Later on, when Destiny and her mum were sitting in the porch of their cabin, she asked Jenny what she thought had happened to Anthony's mum.

'Didn't I tell you?' Jenny asked surprised.

Destiny frowned. 'Tell me what, Mum?' She looked at her mum suspiciously, as understanding began to dawn on her. 'You already know the Greys, don't you!' she said accusingly.

Jenny gave her a rueful smile and admitted, 'I haven't been entirely forthcoming, but I wanted you to make your own decision about the Greys and this place, without being influenced by me.'

As Destiny looked bemused, Jenny hurried on. 'Nicole – that's Anthony's mum – and I used to be very good friends at school. We lost touch for a while and then met up again when you and Anthony were babies.'

'And?'

'And – she got seriously ill.'

'Oh!' Destiny pulled a sympathetic face to show that Jenny didn't need to explain further. 'So how come the ranch in

America?'

'Well, it was something that Nicole always laughingly called her "pipe-dream", that she and Matt would one day own a ranch where all the horses would be trained their way. I think they call it Natural Horsemanship.'

'Oh yeah, I read about that in an article once.'

Jenny raised her eyebrows, but decided she wasn't really surprised. Destiny would struggle through anything to do with animals, no matter how hard or technical.

'Anyway, after she died, Matt decided the only way he could pick up his life again would be to live the dream they had both wanted. That's it!'

'How long ago was that?'

'You were about four, I think. Anthony must be about six months older than you.'

'Funny though,' Destiny mused.

'What is?' asked Jenny.

'Well, Anthony doesn't have an American accent.'

'That's easily explained.' Jenny smiled. 'He goes to boarding school in England.'

'What! And his dad lives over here – and after he's lost his mum as well!'

Destiny was shocked and disgusted in equal measure.

'He stays with his aunt and uncle,' said Jenny firmly. 'And it's not for us to judge why Matt has made that decision.'

Destiny felt rebuffed. 'No,' she said slowly. 'I s'pose not.'

CHAPTER FIVE

Destiny and her mum slept late the next day, exhausted by all the travelling and excitement of the day before. Destiny had only just crawled out of bed and was gazing out of her window, across rolling hills as far as the eye could see when she heard a knock at the door. She opened it. It was Anthony.

'Aunt Kath said you might want breakfast in bed this morning.' He grinned.

Destiny blushed, realizing she was still in her pyjamas.

'Er, thanks.'

Jenny appeared. 'Breakfast, we are being spoilt.'

'Only today.' Anthony seemed to smile whenever he talked. 'Usually people either have breakfast up at the house, or you'll find you've got cereals and bread and stuff in the kitchen.' He turned to Destiny. 'I'll show you the stables when you've finished, if you like.'

She marvelled at how he chatted so easily to people he hardly knew, but she supposed he'd had to get used to it.

'Thanks,' she said.

The yard was immaculate. Destiny wasn't sure what she'd expected, but she wondered how it was possible to keep everything so clean.

Anthony clearly adored the horses. He knew all their names and every single one whickered softly at his approach, as though greeting a friend.

'Do they stay in their boxes all the time?'

The horses seemed content enough, but Destiny thought it must be a very dreary life if they were standing around cooped up all day.

If Anthony thought it was a stupid question, he didn't show it. He explained that they were only in their stables because the farrier was coming. Usually, the horses were out grazing unless it got unbearably hot in the afternoon; then they came in to rest.

It didn't seem to matter whether Destiny knew anything about horses or not. She felt she could ask Anthony anything and he wouldn't mind.

'What if it rains?'

'We rug them up and they stay out, unless there's a hurricane or something.'

'That doesn't seem very nice.' She frowned.

'What you have to remember...' and for once, Anthony looked serious, '...is that horses aren't human. They don't see things the way we do. For them it's normal and right to be outside, whatever the weather. The only reason we put rugs on is because we do unnatural things like clipping them.

(Destiny was to find that thinking like a horse would become a big part of her life. It was certainly something she would hear again and again during her stay.)

In no time at all it was lunchtime. Whether it was the fresh air, they didn't know, but both Destiny and her mum were absolutely ravenous. However, there seemed to be enough food to feed an army, with so much choice it was hard to make decisions and not just pig out on everything.

'They won't be able to find horses big enough to carry us after two weeks,' groaned Jenny. Destiny grinned. She realized she was actually very happy.

Riding, it turned out, would take place in the mornings and early evenings, because it was too hot during the middle of the day. Destiny felt butterflies crowding like bad-tempered kick boxers inside her stomach. This was the part she wasn't looking forward to. When it came to saddling up time she stood miserably at the entrance to the yard, watching her mum chat animatedly to one of the ranch hands, Harvey. There was no sign of Anthony, a fact which half pleased and half dismayed her.

'You must be Destiny,' a low, pleasant voice said from behind her.

She jumped and span round, only to be confronted by a shirt front that seemed to extend for miles, until she nearly got a crick in her neck looking up at the tallest man she thought she had ever seen.

It turned out that this was Merlin, which of course immediately made Destiny think of a magician. He had been assigned to teach her to ride, while her mum went out for a hack with Harvey. Well he'll *have* to be a magician to teach me to ride, she thought glumly. Her legs already felt like jelly and she wasn't even on yet!

Merlin chatted away while he was tacking up, and Destiny began to relax a little. He told her that, before long, she would learn to tack up herself. *Yeah, right,* she thought. It seemed impossible that she would ever remember the name of the hundreds of bits that needed 'cinching up' or whatever, let alone do the right thing with them.

'Okay,' he said at last. He gave Destiny a long look. 'Nervous?'

'Terrified,' she agreed.

'Right oh, then, there's only one thing for it.' He produced a small bottle from his pocket. 'Just a small swig, it will help.'

Destiny looked doubtful. Merlin laughed at the concerned look on her face.

'I don't think your mum would be very impressed if I poisoned you,' he said gently. 'It's an herbal remedy to soothe your nerves and I already checked it out with your mum, just in case.'

Destiny was well aware how important it was to be careful of drinks you were offered by someone you didn't know well; she figured, in this particular situation, she was most likely quite safe. She took a small mouthful from the bottle. It wasn't especially nice tasting, but it felt warm and comforting as it went down.

The first ten minutes of her lesson had nothing to do with sitting on the horse, whose name was Wasp. Merlin explained that Destiny needed to get to know the horse and find out what kind of mood he was in before she got on his back. When she looked surprised, he told her that horses had moods the same as people and they felt better about you if they got to know you before you started getting too personal.

Merlin made Destiny stroke Wasp gently but firmly (they don't like being tickled; that's what flies do) all over. She was uncertain about picking up his feet, but was nonetheless amazed by how easy it was to touch him down his legs and everywhere. She even found his 'itchy spot', just under his mane. Merlin showed her how, when she scratched Wasp's itchy spot, he scrunched up his top lip and wiggled it about – a sign of real pleasure.

'Now he's ready for you to get aboard,' said Merlin.

Destiny took a deep breath. This was the bit she had been dreading.

'But first...'

Uh, oh, thought Destiny, what now? But she realized that, so far, Wasp had been as good as gold and Merlin hadn't asked her to do anything she couldn't cope with.

What Merlin wanted her to do seemed a bit strange at first. She had to stand on a block, put her foot in the stirrup and then just stand up so that she was twisting kind of forward over the saddle.

'Look him in the eye as you mount,' Merlin told her, 'and give him a pat once you're up there. It's like saying "please" before you sit on him. Courteous like.'

It had never occurred to Destiny that she might need to be courteous to a horse, but the way Merlin explained it made a lot of sense.

Wasp stood patiently while she hopped up and down a few times, so swinging her leg over to sit on him seemed an easy step when it happened. Merlin showed her how to sit comfortably and how to hold the reins. The horse's headgear was nothing like Destiny had seen before. Merlin called it a Bosal. It felt like there was nothing between Wasp and shooting off (and Destiny with him) apart from a bit of rope.

'Okay, are we ready to have a walk?'

So far so good, but now the prospect of Wasp moving seemed an insurmountable hurdle.

'What we do with horses,' explained Merlin, 'if they're scared, is just ask them to make a tiny try, just to see how it goes. You think you can do that?'

'Okay.' Her voice sounded very quivery.

Merlin chatted away a bit more and then suddenly said, 'There!'

'What?'

'There, that was a step.'

'Really?'

'Sure, want to do it again?'

'Okay.' This time her voice was a bit firmer. Destiny definitely felt Wasp take the next step and she decided it wasn't really all that scary. Before long, Merlin was leading her all around the corral and they were chatting away like old friends.

Then, with a jolt, Destiny became aware that Merlin was no longer holding Wasp. She squeaked. Merlin smiled.

'You've been like that for the last ten minutes!' He chuckled. Destiny relaxed.

'Great, that's a real good note to finish on,' he said happily.

Destiny found, to her complete surprise, that she was sorry the lesson was over.

CHAPTER SIX

Snake was so called, because he had a snake's tail trailing in a sinister kind of way from the small of his back. It was about four foot long and he kept it coiled in a leather pouch that hung at his side. He had learnt to use it quite effectively. It made a sharp stinging whip and he had even been known to strangle Creations with it. A formidable weapon!

A young girl had drawn him many years ago. Crevitos, who had very much liked the design, had long since discovered that he could produce Creations of his own, simply by drawing them. He had designed a number of them, based on a similar theme: human beings with one simple animal attribute – which could be deadly.

There was only one snag with Crevitos's Creations and a rather large one, he had to admit. They were weak. Because he himself was someone's creation (though he shuddered to admit it to himself) he simply did not have the power behind his imagination that human beings had. And, despite his warnings, and despite a huge number of deaths amongst Doomland's population, there were *still* some who defied him. And those very Creations who defied him had discovered his own Creations' weakness.

But he would find them. He would find these traitors and when he did...

Crevitos stretched, smiled and hummed a little to himself. If all went according to plan, he would double, treble, maybe even quadruple his strength and then, *then* his Creations would not be so easily overcome.

Then HE Crevitos, the greatest ruler any world had ever known, would be invincible.

CHAPTER SEVEN

A small group of people stood at the corral fence watching events with a variety of emotions ranging from horror to awe. Merlin was having trouble with a youngster. At least he didn't *look* very troubled, but Destiny didn't think there was anything that could persuade her to stand where he was standing right now.

The youngster, a stallion called Toby, was four years old. He was, apparently, a rescue horse, which meant, so Anthony explained, that some loathsome creep had mistreated the horse. The venom in his voice as he told Destiny this, had quite taken her aback. In three days she had only ever seen him smiling and sunny. But the fact that people could be cruel to animals was a subject that sickened her to the core, so she could totally understand why he felt the way he did.

You wouldn't know Toby was a rescue horse to look at him. It seemed that Anthony's dad had brought him over from England three months previously, at which point he had looked like a walking hat rack. There was no sign of that now. No long curled up hooves, no open, bleeding sores on his face, legs and body. He was plump, shiny and beautifully groomed, but Destiny could see the fear in his face by the way his eyes rolled and his nostrils flared.

As they watched, he reared high above Merlin's head, front hooves thrashing ominously close to the man standing patiently before him. Destiny marvelled that Merlin could stand so still and so apparently unconcerned.

'What's he doing?' she breathed into Anthony's ear, terrified of making any noise that might upset Toby further.

'He'll wait it out,' Anthony whispered back. 'You watch, in a bit Toby will realize that Merlin's not threatening him and that rearing isn't getting him anywhere. Then he'll stop.'

Destiny watched. It seemed like an age passed as Toby

plunged and reared around Merlin and she watched with dread, expecting at any moment to see half a tonne of horse come crashing down on Merlin's head.

Then it was over!

Toby stood still, his coat matted with sweat, eyes still rolling but, nonetheless, quiet. Merlin reached forward very slowly and rubbed the stallion's neck. After a couple of minutes, he began to lead Toby gently around, circling first one way and then the other.

'Watch now,' Anthony mouthed sideways, although his gaze was concentrated entirely on Merlin and the young horse.

'Look at Toby's eyes and mouth.'

Destiny looked, not entirely sure what she was watching for. As she observed, Toby's head dropped.

'There!' Anthony sounded triumphant. 'See him licking and chewing?'

Sure enough, out came Toby's tongue. He seemed to lick his lips for a bit and then make a motion as though he were chewing grass.

'What does that mean?' Destiny whispered tentatively, afraid of breaking whatever spell it was that held Anthony in its grip.

'He's thinking!'

'Who is?'

'Toby. Look at his eyes; see how they're softening!'

And Destiny could see. It surprised her how obvious the body language was and yet it would never have occurred to her without Anthony's input. Which was odd, she thought, when it wasn't so different from what she'd learnt about cats and dogs. Of course cats and dogs were predators, not prey animals like horses, but fear was fear whichever way you looked at it!

From that point on the tension was gone. Merlin continued to walk Toby around, halt him, back him up and give him lots of praise. Anthony explained that it was the first time Toby had been in the corral.

'He's got a lot of hang ups, you know, like mental baggage, but Merlin's really amazing. He'll get Toby right.'

Destiny was inclined to agree. She thought what she had just seen was the most amazing, moving, magical event she had ever witnessed. Toby was now following Merlin around without a lead rope, stopping when Merlin stopped, turning when he turned.

'It's like he really *is* a magician,' she whispered to herself.

Anthony caught her mutter and grinned.

'He's what's generally known as a "horse whisperer", but there's not a lot of whispering going on. Mostly it's about psychology. Horses are pack animals and they're looking for a herd leader. That way they feel safe.'

Understanding kicked in and Destiny beamed at Anthony.

'So *that's* what Merlin's done, he's become herd leader!' Destiny was fascinated. 'Whoa, that's incredible!' She gazed thoughtfully at Toby who was now grazing by the side of the corral, back leg resting, as though he hadn't a care in the world.

CHAPTER EIGHT

It was amazing how it had only taken Destiny a week to shake off her fear of sitting on a horse. Now she woke up in the morning, excitement fluttering in her stomach at the prospect of riding for a few hours.

On this particular morning she woke with an equal measure of eagerness and apprehension. For the past four days she had watched, fascinated, as Merlin worked his magic on Toby. She had also been more than a little impressed to see Anthony handling Toby with much the same sort of calm assurance as Merlin himself.

Toby was no midget at sixteen hands and he towered above Anthony. Once or twice, Destiny had seen Toby spook while Anthony was leading him around, skittering sideways and throwing his head up in the air. Even with her newfound confidence, Destiny knew it would have terrified her. Anthony seemed to just calmly let out his lead rope a little, moving, so Destiny noticed, *with* the horse rather than away from him, careful to keep out of harm's way but not seeming at all afraid. Then, when Toby settled, as he inevitably did, Anthony would talk softly to him and stroke his head, neck and ears.

Today was going to be a special one for Destiny. Merlin had said he thought she might be ready to canter, a prospect which half delighted and half terrified her. Destiny felt too queasy to eat breakfast, but Jenny insisted she had an apple, as riding could be strenuous work. As they walked up towards the yard, Destiny looked tentatively at her mum.

'How is it,' she began, 'that you can really, really want to do something but feel terrified at the same time?'

'I don't know, I think it's a bit like actors who feel sick every time they have to go on stage. I take it it's the riding you're talking about?'

'Merlin says I can canter today!' Destiny blurted out.

'And you want to, but you don't?'

'Something like that!'

Jenny gave her daughter's arm a squeeze. 'You'll love it. It's much more comfortable than trotting!'

Destiny was glad her mum hadn't tried to explain away the nerves, or suggested that she breathe deeply or something. Jenny's matter of fact certainty that Destiny would enjoy it was more helpful than anything else she could have said.

Tacking up Wasp was becoming second nature now, but Destiny was so nervous she kept fumbling with everything. Merlin as usual was totally patient. Having led Wasp around a bit, backed him up, flexed his head left and right and made a fuss of him, Destiny prepared to mount. Wordlessly and without so much as a flicker of a smile, Merlin handed her the herbal remedy. She reached out her hand to take it and then stopped. Trapping her bottom lip with her teeth, Destiny took in a huge breath and then let it out slowly. She shook her head. Merlin, in return, gave her a curt nod of approval and tucked the bottle back into his pocket. That look felt better than any amount of remedy and Destiny placed her foot firmly into the stirrup before springing lightly onto Wasp's back.

From then on, nerves forgotten, Destiny went through the exercises she was beginning to know so well, with quiet determination. After a while, Merlin asked her to bring Wasp into the middle of the corral to have breather.

'Now,' he said nonchalantly, stroking Wasp's neck gently, 'we're going to try something a little bit different, but I'll be right here with you.'

By now Destiny had learnt to trust Merlin. She knew he never asked her to do anything he didn't think she was capable of. Obviously they weren't going to canter yet. Even with Merlin's long stride, she guessed it would be impossible for him to 'stay with her' in canter. Intrigued and also slightly disappointed,

Destiny said, 'Okay' in as cheery a voice as she could muster. Merlin raised an eyebrow and smiled a little as though he had guessed her thoughts.

'Okay, we'll start this slow, but I want you to tell me straight away if you get scared or you don't like it, or whatever – promise?'

'Promise!'

From his Doctor Who like pockets, Merlin produced a dark-blue silk scarf, which, he explained, he was going to tie around Destiny's eyes as a blindfold. It felt supremely odd sitting on top of a horse with a blindfold on!

'Okay?' Merlin's voice sounded louder and crisper somehow, now that she didn't have her vision.

'Fine.' Destiny tried a smile, but even that felt strange; sort of disjointed.

First of all, Merlin led Wasp around at a quiet walk. He kept his hand resting lightly on Destiny's ankle so that she knew he was still there. He kept talking too, which was reassuring. He told Destiny just to sit, relax and go with the movement. Walking was fine, but then Merlin suggested a trot. Destiny wondered where all this was leading, but she murmured her consent. To begin with she clung nervously to the front of the saddle. Then she found that, in a funny sort of way, it was easier to pick up on Wasp's rhythm without her vision. She began to relax and rather enjoy the feeling.

'That's good, real good.' Merlin's voice came from a slight distance and Destiny became aware that she couldn't feel the pressure of his hand on her ankle any more. She smiled to herself. It was just like her first lesson. Merlin told her to bring Wasp down to walk and then halt. She felt him pat her ankle.

'Okay, that was the easy bit. I'm not going to hold you or Wasp, but you'll be completely safe. Do you trust me?'

'You know I do!'

'Just sit. The way you have been. Don't *do* anything, okay?

Wasp's done this before. He knows the score. If you touch your hat, we'll stop!'

To Destiny's surprise, a slow melodious tune began to drift across the corral.

Wasp stood still.

'Now,' Merlin said softly, 'forget everything you've learnt about riding; just feel the rhythm and move with the music. There's no one else to see. Just feel it!'

Destiny felt a hot rush of blood stain her cheeks and was instantly furious with herself. It didn't matter if anyone else was there, *she* couldn't see so it didn't matter.

The music grew louder and time trickled to a standstill. She was in a world all by herself. Deprived of sight and all sound apart from the melody she was hearing, she began to sway with the music.

Gently.

Shifting from one seat bone to the other.

Slowly.

Rhythmically.

And Wasp moved with her.

A small gasp escaped her lips, but the feeling was magic! Wasp walked in time with Destiny, as Destiny moved in time with the music.

With no sudden change, the music flowed into a faster pace. Destiny was completely immersed now; totally absorbed in the sound around her. Wasp quickened beneath her and rippled like silk into a trot. Destiny moved with him, hardly aware that anything had changed. She had no idea where Wasp was going, but it didn't matter. The beat, the sensation, engrossed her.

Now the music was changing again. This time a three-beat rhythm. Destiny's hips swung with the motion.

And Wasp cantered!

She knew. Deep inside her, part of her knew what he was doing, but she was too absorbed to register it fully.

Adrenaline coursed through her. The feeling was electric...

Destiny moved with the rhythm that Wasp had relaxed into, totally swayed by the music and feeling of power underneath her.

The music slowed gently and so did the pace until finally Wasp glided out of his canter to...trot...trot...trot...trot... waaalk...

The music stopped.

Wasp stopped.

Silence.

Stillness.

Destiny came to.

A wild cheering and clapping erupted and Destiny whipped the scarf off to see half a dozen people, including Anthony, whooping by the corral fence.

She looked at Merlin feeling an uncontrollable, foolish grin on her face and saw it mirrored there on his.

'Beautiful,' he croaked and she was stunned to see that his eyes were full of tears.

'Beautiful!'

CHAPTER NINE

Boff shivered in the darkness.

Life, he thought, would be so much better for all these Creations in another dimension than life on Doomland. Anything would be better than the constant wearing grind of working in one of Crevitos's pits and even here, in the North, he had forgotten how hard and bleak and cheerless an existence they led.

Crevitos had found that Doomland had an abundant supply of some sort of stuff called 'diamond'. It looked, when the workers dug it out of the ground, like lumps of dirt. When it was cleaned up, it looked pretty enough, but Boff could see no real value to it at all. However, Crevitos demanded that thousands of Creations toil in the mines, digging up these apparently worthless lumps of rock. It was hard, heavy, dangerous work, made no easier by the lashing of whips by Crevitos's spiteful henchmen.

Creations were not strong by nature and many faltered and disintegrated every day. Many more were left mutilated or scarred by the merciless blows dealt out by Crevitos's chosen few.

However, all creatures look for hope even in the direst adversity and Creations were no exception. A small society of them had got together and had managed to elude Crevitos's constantly roving eye. They had, over some time, gathered what meagre provisions they could muster, hiding them carefully from Crevitos's corrupt band of supporters. Then, one moonless night, they had set off for the barren wastes of northern Doomland, where no sane Creation – not even insane ones like Crevitos – would choose to live.

The journey had been arduous, but they had finally found a place where they could eke out a tough and watchful living.

Every so often, a small party of these liberated Creations

would make the long journey back to central Doomland and recruit another handful of Creations, who were only too ready to clutch at any straw to be free of Crevitos's tyranny. In this way, they could save at least a few of their friends from drudgery, despair and most likely, death.

Now, however, the Eldons (as they liked to call themselves) of the Liberated Creation Party were getting worried. The number of Creations who had escaped Crevitos's domination was rapidly growing. It was becoming harder and harder to remain hidden. Not only that, but Crevitos was well aware of their existence and they were increasingly worried that one of their new recruits might well turn out to be one of his escalating army of spies.

They called a council. It was agreed, with much sadness and despair that, for the moment, there could be no more rescue parties. It was time for the group to find somewhere safer to live. It had long been common knowledge that there were other dimensions, other worlds than Doomland, but how you might travel to these other places had remained a great mystery.

Until now!

A small figure stood up hesitantly and raised a tentative hand. 'I only arrived back here last night,' he said quietly, 'and I didn't come from the mines, I came from a place called Emajen. I can show you how to get there!'

CHAPTER TEN

After her amazing experience on Wasp, Destiny hadn't looked back. Her confidence had soared and Merlin at last had deemed her ready to go out on her first hack. She loved it, not least because she, Merlin, Anthony and her mum went out as a foursome. She was a bit uncertain at first – she suddenly felt very vulnerable being up on Wasp in all that open space – but Wasp was as good as gold and Destiny soon relaxed.

On the way back, Merlin and Jenny trotted off on a different track to jump over some small fences. Anthony and Destiny rode the short route home together. They chatted away easily. Destiny and her mum had been there for ten days, but it seemed to Destiny as though she had been there forever. The bond she had forged with Anthony made her feel like she had known him all her life.

They were in sight of the ranch when there was a vivid flash and a tremendous boom of thunder. From seemingly nowhere, sheets of water cascaded mercilessly out of a rapidly darkening sky. At that moment, Toby newly backed and far less experienced than Wasp, snorted, threw his head up and thrust his front legs wildly up into the air.

Wasp started dancing, but only on the spot and Destiny watched with horror as Toby plunged down and then reared again, a valiant Anthony clinging desperately to his mane.

By now, they were all soaked through. The lightning seared again, shooting streaks of white fire in jagged lines towards the earth. Toby screamed when the next thunderclap boomed. Hooves flailing, he soared upwards, standing almost upright. Anthony had no chance. The rain had made everything so slippery that he was thrown up in the air like a rag doll and Destiny could only watch helplessly, as he catapulted through space to land with a sickening thud, only millimetres from

Toby's thrashing hooves.

But before Destiny had time to react, Anthony was on his feet, grabbing for Toby's reins. The horse was wild by now, eyes rolling in their sockets, nostrils flared. Mercifully, the storm chose this moment to abate, as quickly as it had arisen. Toby bounced; alternately raising his forelegs and then his hind legs in the air. Anthony's face had taken on the expression that Destiny was becoming well used to, one of calm concentration. He had hold of the reins at their furthest point to avoid being struck by the horse's hooves and every time that Toby tossed his head, Anthony stood firm, not pulling at him, but not allowing the horse to jerk away.

Gradually, after what seemed an age, Toby stopped prancing. His eyes still showed their whites and he snorted heavily. He was trembling all over, but at last he stood still. Anthony stepped slowly in towards his shoulder, talking soothingly to him.

'Good lad, good lad, only a silly old storm. You're fine, you're okay, good lad.'

Gently he stroked Toby's neck. If Toby shied or danced again, Anthony stopped stroking and ceased talking. As soon as Toby stood still, the stroking and soft murmuring resumed – a reward for Toby's calm behaviour.

At last Toby's head dropped. He licked his lips and snuffled softly into Anthony's hand.

Destiny drew a deep breath, only now aware that she had been holding it for some moments. At last Anthony looked at her. She was shocked by how pale his face was and was suddenly aware that he was holding his left arm very awkwardly.

'Do you think you could manage to get back to the house without me?' Anthony asked quietly, with no expectation, but Destiny could see the pain in his eyes. 'It's not far. I'll have to start walking Toby back. He's too keyed up. He won't stand me on his back just now!'

'Of course I can!' she said, far more bravely than she felt. 'I'll be as quick as I can!'

'Don't hurry, take it steady. Wasp will look after you.'

Destiny niggled at Wasp with her legs, as Merlin had taught her to do and Wasp, with the merest shake of his head, strode forwards. There was a dirt track just ahead that led directly to the corral. Fighting the urge to make Wasp go faster, Destiny felt like it was taking her forever to get to the ranch; one of those moments where one mile seems more like a thousand!

She found herself feeling conflicting emotions, concern for Anthony mixed with a strange combination of fear and exhilaration at actually riding this horse, on her own, out on the deserted track.

Fortunately, it didn't stay deserted for long. Merlin and Jenny had headed for home with the first thunderclap, only to realize that there was no sign of the other two. They had immediately turned tail and were already halfway back up the track, when they saw Destiny, bedraggled and looking like a very small, lost ghost, plodding towards them.

Destiny felt like crying with relief, but was determined not to be weak when Anthony had shown so much courage. Somewhat breathlessly she gabbled what had happened, turning in the saddle and waving frantically back in the direction she had come from.

Wordlessly, Merlin put his strong arm around her waist and helped her to slide off Wasp's back. Handing the reins to Jenny, he turned and strode swiftly up the track.

CHAPTER ELEVEN

Destiny sat by the fire, wrapped in a blanket, with a cup of hot chocolate cradled in her hands, feeling much better. Every so often she shivered, although she wasn't really cold.

'Shock!' her mum said, which wasn't very surprising.

Merlin had discovered Anthony staggering towards the track. He was virtually out on his feet, sheer determination keeping him going. He'd since been whipped off to the nearest hospital, forty miles away and the news had come back that he had most likely cracked some ribs and had broken his right arm.

Four days later, Destiny sat watching Anthony schooling Toby in the round pen. Anthony's arm was in a cast, but he had insisted vehemently that he could still school the horses on the ground even if he couldn't ride. It wouldn't actually have surprised Destiny if he had demanded to be allowed to ride one handed.

Toby stopped cantering around and came across to the middle of the pen where Anthony was standing. He lowered his head for a stroke and Anthony patted him affectionately.

Destiny jumped down from the fence and walked over to them. She couldn't quite believe this was her last day. So much had happened in a fortnight and she had learnt so much. In some ways, she felt she was a completely different person going home, to the one who had arrived fourteen days ago.

In two hours' time she would be heading for the airport, going back to a life she could hardly imagine she had ever lived. All that seemed real to her was what happened on this ranch and the amazing way that Merlin, Anthony and the others handled the horses. Destiny smiled a little to herself.

'Penny for them?' queried Anthony.

Destiny shook herself out of her daydream.

'I was just thinking...'

'I guessed that,' Anthony teased gently.

'Shut up! I was thinking how quickly the time's gone. Going home will be really strange!'

'Yeah, for me too.'

'You *are* home!' Destiny teased back.

'You know what I mean...we'll keep in touch though, won't we?' Anthony said, slightly embarrassed. 'I'd really like to!' he finished hurriedly.

'How about we email every Sunday?' Destiny suggested.

'Okay, you're on! How about you hose Toby down and put him out for me?'

Destiny hesitated just for a second; Toby could be a handful. But Anthony instilled her with the same confidence that Merlin did and Destiny knew that he was offering her a huge compliment by entrusting Toby to her.

'Sure,' she agreed lightly, and Anthony's answering smile made her glow all over with happiness.

* * *

Many hugs and best wishes later, Destiny found herself ready to board the plane home. She was about to turn off her mobile, when a well-timed text message made her jump.

WASP MISSES U

I DO 2

A X

Much to her consternation, Destiny felt tears sting her eyes. Carefully saving the text, she turned off her mobile and didn't cry until Mum was breathing in gentle sleep beside her on the long journey home.

CHAPTER TWELVE

Sebastian Quentin Isaiah Brown was a very lucky little boy, born with the proverbial silver spoon in his mouth. In other words, his parents were loaded. However, although fortune smiled broadly upon Sebastian until about the age of two, fate had other ideas in store for him. In fact, when Sebastian Quentin Isaiah Brown was no more than two years, three months and six days old, his mother and father decided to go on a safari holiday. Thinking that this was maybe not a terribly congenial environment for a two-year-old boy, they left him in the charge of Nanny, with strict instructions that he should eat his vegetables and have a walk every day.

What happened next is too horrible to describe, except to say that Sebastian Quentin Isaiah Brown's parents were caught up in a rather unfortunate incident involving a stampeding herd of wildebeest. In no more than a few earth-shattering seconds, it was all over and the Browns were no more!

When the news reached Nanny, she was taking Sebastian for his daily constitutional in the park (as instructed) and she was so shocked, she fainted dead away.

Poor Nanny was getting on a bit and, much as she loved Sebastian, she really didn't feel able to take him into her sole care. Since Sebastian didn't have any other relatives he found himself officially an orphan.

Being a very appealing little boy, with a mop of unruly, dark hair and big, soulful, brown eyes, Sebastian was quick to find foster parents. However fortune had decided to turn its back on our poor little orphan again. Of all the hundreds and thousands of lovely, caring parents Sebastian could have had, he found himself lodged with Mr and Mrs M. Eanie.

By the time Sebastian was seven years old, he had become heartily sick of scrubbing floors, washing dishes and cleaning out the pigs.

One fresh, chilly Christmas day, Mr and Mrs M. Eanie decided they were going to visit their grown-up daughter in a neighbouring village. They left Sebastian with a list of chores long enough to keep him out of trouble all day and a chunk of bread 'to stop the little brat from whingeing!'

As well as pigs, Mr and Mrs M. Eanie also had chickens on their farm. One of Sebastian's chores was to collect the eggs, which actually he didn't mind too much doing. The hen house was at least warm and the chickens were friendly and soft to stroke.

Sebastian sat for a moment in the chicken run, stroking his favourite hen, who would lovingly rub her head against his hand, when suddenly he noticed one of the smallest hens trying to squeeze through a tiny hole under the wire fence. Horrified, he leapt up, knowing that if the bird escaped he, Sebastian, would probably end up sleeping in the coal shed or worse. Scooping up the adventurous little hen, he gently set it down next to its friends and hurriedly scraped some dirt into the hole to fill it up.

That was when he had his idea.

Whooping with joy, his legs moving like pistons, Sebastian Quentin Isaiah Brown ran away!

CHAPTER THIRTEEN

Sebastian's eyes almost popped out of his head with amazement. He had never known there could be so many people all together in one place. Hunger had driven him towards this bustle of humanity and he marvelled at the whirl of colours and noises that filled the spaces around him. All he could remember was being on the pig farm. He had long since forgotten his real parents and walks in the park with Nanny. Now here he was in a place where people thronged and milled about, shouting and laughing with children scrapping and chasing each other.

There were stalls, like the ones he'd seen on market days with Mr M. Eanie, but much bigger and more colourful, selling everything from brightly coloured confectionary to thick woollen jackets and much, much more besides.

Then there were the horses, beautiful and shining with riders decked out in their finest: some on board, some leading their mounts around and some seriously brushing already gleaming animals. Of course Sebastian had seen horses before, when the local people met up for a hunt. But only from afar. And these animals were something different altogether.

After a while of feasting his eyes, Sebastian's stomach reminded him of the real reason he had been drawn to this place. More than anything, he was starving. He watched with envy as crowds of people milled around a variety of food stalls. The smells made his mouth water. He watched closely, sure that sooner or later someone would drop something or throw something away that he, Sebastian, could retrieve.

His chance came when a disembodied voice made an announcement over a loudspeaker. A show jumping event was about to take place in ring one. People began to walk quickly towards the place, obviously keen to get a good viewpoint.

As Sebastian watched, a man eating from a carton took one

last chip and threw the remainder in a nearby bin. The bin was practically overflowing, so the carton balanced precariously on the top of the other rubbish. Sebastian gave a quiet inward whoop of joy. Carefully, trying not to draw attention to himself, he scooted over to the bin. With trembling fingers he reached out…

A hand fell heavily on his shoulder. It gripped his tee shirt hard, as he tried to squirm out from underneath it.

'You don't want to eat those!' The voice was gruff, but kindly and it was accompanied by an equally stern but kindly looking face, once Sebastian had twisted around enough to look. It was a hairy face with bushy eyebrows and the biggest beard Sebastian had ever seen. Out of all this furriness, deep set, blue eyes sparkled and there were lines around the man's eyes that made him look smiley, even though, right now, he looked a bit grim.

'Are you really hungry?' the man asked gently.

Sebastian nodded, his eyes taking on a puppy dog sadness that would have melted the stoniest of hearts.

'I'm a stranger, I know,' suggested the man, 'but right now it seems to me that you might well want to take a risk and let a stranger buy you a decent meal rather than eating filthy, germy, cold chips out of a rubbish bin! What do you think?'

With that, he let go of Sebastian's tee shirt and started striding towards a tent with a sign that promised 'GOOD FOOD' and 'HOT BEVERAGES'.

Sebastian hesitated, but not for long. He had never been to school. Nobody had ever given him the talk about saying 'No' to strangers and, right now, food of any description was very appealing. Quickly he trotted after the retreating figure.

The amount of food that appeared on the table made Sebastian's eyes fairly goggle with delight. He couldn't ever remember having had such a huge choice. Hunger overcame uncertainty and, before he'd even had time to stop and think, his hand had shot out of its own accord and reached for a large, satisfying looking piece of pizza, which he stuffed unceremoniously into his mouth almost faster than he could chew.

The man sat watching, taking occasional sips of tea, his only comment, 'Slow down, lad, there's no hurry!'

At last Sebastian sat back and ruefully eyed a large jacket potato and several cakes that he was too stuffed to consume.

'Don't worry.' The man smiled. 'You can take them with you.'

Replete at last, Sebastian remembered the manners that had been so drilled into him in his dim, distant past by Nanny that they were second nature.

'Thank you…er…Sir?' he said hesitantly, wiping his mouth on his sleeve (which was definitely *not* something Nanny had taught him to do).

'I'm not a "Sir",' chuckled the man. 'Most people call me Prof.'

'Why do they call you that? It's very short!'

'Well you're right, of course. It *is* short. Actually it's short for professor.'

'So really, Professor is your name,' said Sebastian curiously.

'Not exactly. Professor is what I am, or at least what I used to be a long time ago,' the Prof said in a slightly wistful voice.

'Oh!' Sebastian had rather lost interest in this conversation and was eyeing up a large chocolate muffin. He debated whether he should squeeze it down now, or save it for later. The Prof asking him a question interrupted his train of thought.

'So what should I call *you*, young man?'

'My name is Sebastian, Quentin, Isaiah, Brown,' replied the little boy proudly. The Eanies had laughed out loud about Sebastian's name and had used it to taunt him with whenever they were feeling particularly mean (which was quite a lot of the time). Sebastian himself felt it sounded rather grand.

'Well,' the professor mused, '*that's* very long! I think perhaps I should call you SQUIB.'

Sebastian considered a moment, his bright little brain processing what he had been able to glean of letters and words.

He mulled over the professor's suggestion and it occurred to him that SQUIB was indeed a rather shorter way of calling him all of his names at once, names of which he was very proud. A bit like the professor being called Prof. And although Sebastian didn't really know what a professor was, it seemed to him that it too might be something rather grand. Like his name.

Having reasoned thus, he looked at the Prof solemnly and said slowly, 'Yes, I think I like that.'

'Then Squib you shall be.' The Prof laughed.

Squib looked at the friendly face before him. Apart from asking his name, the Prof hadn't questioned him about anything at all. Squib suddenly felt an overwhelming desire to confide in the only person he could ever remember being kind to him.

'Prof, can I tell you a secret?' he asked in a rush.

The Prof at once looked serious, but only nodded slightly, so Squib hurried on.

'I've run away!' he blurted out.

The Prof nodded again. Such an understanding nod, it seemed to Squib, that suddenly his whole world of misery, living with parents who weren't really his parents (the Eanies had made that abundantly clear) came pouring out in one long, jumbled stream of desperation.

When, at length, Squib ran out of breath, the Prof remained silent for some time. Then he let out a huge sigh, leaned forward in his chair and looked Squib straight in the eye.

'I have a secret too. A very, very, VERY important secret. You trusted me with your secret; can I trust you with mine?'

Squib considered and then rewarded the Prof with an imitation of his own understanding nod, to show that the secret would be safe with him.

The story that unfolded was so amazing, that had Squib been say fourteen years old rather than seven years, five months and seventeen days, he would have most probably assumed that the professor was pulling his leg.

However, life was relatively new to Squib. He hadn't yet learnt that some things should really and truly be impossible. When the Prof had finished his story, he looked expectantly at Squib, waiting for his reaction.

'Is it nice?' Squib asked at last. 'Emajen, I mean.'

'*I* think so,' answered the Prof carefully. 'Squib, do you want to go back to your foster parents?'

'No!' replied Squib firmly.

'Well, I could do with a little help and I could teach you how to read and write properly and about numbers and planets and music and all sorts of interesting things. What do you say?' Suddenly, he glanced at his watch. 'My goodness, I hadn't realized how late it's got. Squib, I have to go!'

Squib looked at the Prof; uncertainty mingled with the beginnings of trust in his new friend flickered in his eyes.

The Prof stood up. He rummaged in his wallet and pulled out some notes.

'Bad of me!' he berated himself. 'You don't know me at all, but perhaps we'll meet again.'

He handed the notes to Squib and held out his hand. 'It's been a pleasure to meet you, young man, and I hope your fortunes change very soon!'

So saying, he turned and strode away.

Squib thought he heard the Prof mutter something like, 'It would have been nice...' but he couldn't be sure.

Squib looked at the money in his hand. He looked at the professor's rapidly retreating figure. Without even realising he had made a decision, he scrunched up the notes in his palm and trotted hurriedly after the professor.

The Prof twisted and turned among the varying stalls. Squib followed silently, like a small shadow, ready to melt away at any moment, should the need arise. At last, they found themselves slightly apart from the bulk of the crowd. This was where the boxes and trailers were parked waiting to take horses and ponies back to their warm, comfortable stables and bulging hay nets.

The Prof disappeared behind a small caravan that looked rather tatty and older than all the other vehicles. Squib peered round the corner, careful not to be seen. The Prof unlocked the caravan door and stepped inside. Cautiously, Squib crept up to the dingy window and raised himself up slowly, so that he could peer into the dimly lit interior.

At first he couldn't see much, but as his eyes grew accustomed to the gloom, he could see the professor lifting something out from underneath the cushioned top of a padded seat. As he lifted this thing, the Prof turned slightly; then Squib could see he was holding some kind of box. Squib could hear him talking to someone, although he couldn't see anyone else there.

As he watched, the Prof produced a strange looking key from his pocket. It seemed to shimmer slightly in the murk, as though it were made of glittering starlight.

What happened next happened so fast that Squib had no time to think.

As the Prof turned the key in the box, the lid sprang open and light seemed to pour out of the box, followed instantly by a splodge of dark. It was like an inkblot that spread out and up until it hovered like a blue-black stain in the middle of the caravan.

Carefully shutting the box, the Prof put the key back in his pocket. Without even glancing round, he stepped purposefully into the pulsating black ooze.

Squib wrenched open the door of the caravan, squealing, 'Wait for me!' He lunged forward into the darkness, just as the blinding light that had filled the caravan sucked back into the dark blot, a mere fraction of a second behind him.

The splodge shrank rapidly and disappeared with a soft *shlurrrp* and the professor and Squib were gone.

CHAPTER FOURTEEN

Flushed and bright eyed, Destiny waited impatiently for Anthony and his dad to appear on the platform. Mr Grey had flown over from America and picked Anthony up from school on his way. Two weeks until Christmas; they would be staying with the Smiths for ten days before going back to Anthony's cousins in Hertfordshire.

Destiny couldn't wait! It was only just over two months since her memorable visit to the ranch in America, but it seemed like a lifetime ago. She and Anthony hadn't missed a single Sunday e-mailing each other, and there was nothing they hadn't talked about over the Net from aliens to school dinners.

Here he was at last. He looked taller than she remembered and Destiny's excitement suddenly wavered. Supposing they'd said everything there was to say over the Internet? What would she talk to him about for ten days?

Anthony caught sight of Destiny and flashed a broad smile. At once her worries vanished. He was the same old Anthony and ten days would barely be long enough!

* * *

That night, they talked on until the wee hours of the morning; quietly so that parents wouldn't come knocking on the door and complaining that it was high time they went to sleep. Destiny wanted to know all about the ranch; how Merlin and Wasp and Toby were doing. Anthony wanted to know how Destiny was getting on with her riding now that she was sharing a pony. They considered what they would do with the days ahead, unaware that unfolding events would plan their holiday for them!

Despite having chatted until late the night before, Destiny awoke early. At first she wondered why she felt so excited. Then she remembered. Today they were going to a big equestrian event. She loved the pre-Christmas horse show. There would be a huge shopping village with stalls you could wander around for hours. Mum always treated them to pizza and then ice cream in the interval.

This year it would be doubly special, because Anthony and his dad would be there.

There was a knock at the door and Anthony's tousled head appeared. Sitting together on Destiny's bed, they discussed the coming event excitedly.

'I can't believe you've never been before!' Destiny said incredulously, for the umpteenth time.

'Well...I...haven't!' Anthony punctuated each word by poking Destiny in the ribs. Destiny giggled. She grabbed her pillow and walloped him with it!

'Right!' he yelled with mock savagery. 'This is war!'

Pillows flew. Destiny giggled so hard she could hardly catch her breath.

Anthony was merciless but, knowing he was stronger than Destiny, never too rough.

The bedroom door flew open.

'Well, kiddies, I hope this isn't an example of how you're going to behave at the show today!' Jenny's face and voice were both stern, but a tiny quivering smirk at one corner of her mouth gave the game away.

Anthony looked crestfallen. 'Sorry, Jenny, I guess we got a bit carried away!'

'Yes, sorry, Mum,' Destiny said meekly, 'but it *was* all Anthony's fault!' So saying, she grasped the opportunity to *whumph* him over the head with her pillow and then collapsed into giggles again.

Jenny feigned despair and rolled her eyes at Anthony. 'You see what I have to put up with?'

Anthony grinned; it was going to be a really good day.

* * *

They arrived in town early, so that they would have time to eat and look around the stalls before the show started.

In the first event, the competitors had to jump six fences in a straight line. The fences got progressively bigger and Destiny and Anthony found they were straining with the riders over every jump; willing the horses not to knock any poles down.

Next they watched with awe as the mounted police riders jumped through hoops of fire and then sailed over fences whilst at the same time removing first their stirrups and then their whole saddles!

'I could never do that!' marvelled Destiny.

'We'll have to give it a try when we get back.' Anthony laughed.

Destiny shot him a 'yeah, right!' look, which was designed to wound at ten paces. Anthony laughed again.

Just before the interval, there was a competition between teams of dogs, who had to run as fast as possible over a group of jumps, flip a ball up in the air by putting a paw on a pedal, catch the ball and then race back again. Destiny screamed herself practically hoarse cheering them on. The only trouble was she wanted them all to win.

They felt thoroughly exhausted by the time the interval came around and definitely in need of a drink.

'Don't be too long!' warned Jenny, 'the interval is only twenty minutes. You don't want to miss the speed stakes.'

'Okay.' Destiny smiled over her shoulder, as she skipped down the stairs, closely followed by Anthony.

It seemed like only thirty seconds later that the announcement came over the tannoy for people to return to their seats for the next event. Destiny and Anthony looked wide-eyed at each other. They had drifted quite some way from their seating block and were somewhere near where the riders went in and out of the arena.

'Let's watch the first couple from here,' suggested Destiny. 'It'll be fun to see them going in and out.'

They watched the first two riders complete the course. The very first was a young girl who rode very fast, making what seemed like impossible swerves and turns in and out of the jumps. The audience *ooohed* and *aaahed,* caught up in the thrill of the round. There was a taut silence as she approached the last fence...then came a roar of approval as she cleared it and raced through the finishing line.

'Wow!' exclaimed Anthony, impressed. 'The rest of them will have to go some to beat that!'

They decided to start watching the third rider and then to make their way back to their seats.

'Gosh, he looks grumpy,' remarked Destiny, as the man rode in.

'His horse doesn't look too happy either!' replied Anthony, grimly. 'He'll have trouble with this one, you watch.'

Sure enough, the horse bounced around the arena shaking its head wildly and pulling hard, as it rushed uncontrollably over the first two fences. At the third fence, they seemed to reach it all wrong. The horse flung its head up in the air and just seemed to plough right through the jump, instead of taking off. Its rider was almost unseated. When he regained his balance, he had a thunderous look on his face.

He whacked the horse hard, twice, with his whip. Anthony tutted, and muttered under his breath, 'That wasn't the horse's fault!'

Two more jumps were trashed and, by now, Destiny could see that the horse was getting wild. The rider gave the commentator a grim smile and touched his hat to show he was retiring. He made a great show of patting his horse and the crowd clapped appreciatively.

Anthony however, was not so impressed.

'Come on,' he said, tugging at Destiny's sleeve.

'Where are we going?' she asked, surprised.

'I want to see what happens to that horse when the crowd aren't watching,' he said seriously, leading her towards the area where the show jumpers and grooms milled around.

'We can't go in there!' hissed Destiny. 'Look, there are guards at the entrance.'

'It's easy, just watch.'

Anthony waited until a group of people were making their way towards the gate.

'Come on,' he whispered again, and dragged Destiny until they were both walking at the side of the group farthest from the guards. As they approached the gate, Anthony said, 'As we go through the gate, laugh!' He started telling her a funny story about one of the horses on the ranch. He'd got to the bit where one of the ranch hands was being dragged around the yard hanging for dear life on to the horse's tail, when they passed through the entrance.

It *was* a funny story and he told it well.

Destiny forgot she was supposed to be pretending and laughed out loud. The guards glanced at each other and grinned.

Then they were through.

Once they were out of earshot, Destiny gasped, 'That was really sneaky!'

'Not really, you just have to not *be* guilty and then you don't *look* guilty, so nobody gets the wrong vibes.'

'That's so cool. I'm gonna remember that one,' she said firmly.

As they rounded a corner, there was a commotion going on. Without a word, they both began to run. In the centre of the outside arena were the rider and horse they had just seen competing. A small crowd had gathered to see what was going on.

Pushing their way to the front, Anthony and Destiny were in time to see a smallish rotund figure, face the colour of ripe tomatoes, jabbing an angry finger at the sneering rider.

'You're a disgrace,' yelled tomato face. 'You shouldn't be allowed *near* a 'orse, let alone ride one!'

The horse itself stood slightly apart, sweating and visibly trembling. Anthony grabbed Destiny's arm and pointed towards its flanks with a shaking finger. Destiny clapped her hand over her mouth in horror. There were clear welts to be seen, some of them showing speckles of red.

As they watched, an angry looking official strode towards the scene intent on sorting out the commotion. At first he started shouting at Tomato Face, demanding to know, 'What the hell he thought he was doing,' and 'Who the hell he thought he was!'

Instead of shouting back, Tomato Face instantly clammed up and pointed an accusing finger at the subdued horse.

Now it was the official's turn to go red in the face. He rounded sharply on the rider with a look of furious disgust on his face.

'Be assured,' he said quietly, 'that we take such incidents very seriously. There will be a disciplinary hearing. I will see to it personally!'

The rider, who was now not looking quite so sure of himself, began to protest.

'Look here…it's not how it looks…this man…'

The official ignored him and pushed him to one side, ordering that the horse should immediately be taken to the duty vet to have its wounds looked at.

It was over.

The rider gave Tomato Face – who by now was grinning all over his face – a venomous look and hissed, 'I won't forget this!'

'I should 'ope not,' remarked Tomato Face cheerily. He turned and strode away.

With lots of shakings of heads, the crowd began to melt away too.

'Quick,' breathed Anthony in Destiny's ear, 'let's go after him.'

'Who?'

'The man who was complaining.' He was already hurrying her in the direction that Tomato Face had taken. They followed him out of the arena and back into the shopping village. Anthony was walking so fast, Destiny had to trot to keep up with him.

'Why...are...we...following him,' she asked breathlessly.

'I recognize him from somewhere and anyway, I want to say thank you.'

'What for?'

'For giving that horrible man a piece of his mind AND getting him in trouble with the authorities.'

Now that Anthony mentioned it, Destiny too thought that she recognized the retreating figure, but she couldn't place from where.

They had nearly reached the gate to their own seating area when they lost sight of him.

'Oh, bother,' said Anthony vehemently.

They scanned the crowd for some sign of him, but he'd gone.

'Where did he go? One minute he's there and the next he's vanished!'

'Never mind,' said Destiny. 'I guess we ought to get back to Mum anyway. She's probably going ballistic by now.'

'Yeah, you're right,' sighed Anthony.

They turned into the gateway.

CHAPTER FIFTEEN

A hand shot out from under the dark stairway. It grabbed Anthony's coat and jerked him backwards into the dim recess.

'Hey!' yelled Destiny, but her cry was drowned out by a roar of excitement from the crowd above. She plunged forward into the gloom and ran smack into Anthony.

'Oof!' they both exclaimed at the same time.

The light from a small torch pierced the murk. It wavered rather wildly, as the short, stocky figure they had been following apologized over and over for dragging Anthony so unceremoniously into the dark nook.

'I'm so sorry,' he uttered for the tenth time. 'I really 'ope you weren't too scared, only I didn't want anyone to see, see?'

'You didn't want anyone to see what?' asked Destiny puzzled.

'Shhh,' said the man mysteriously, putting a finger to his lips, even though nobody could possibly hear them against the chatter and clatter of the crowds all around.

Anthony and Destiny glanced at each other questioningly.

Then Anthony said politely, 'I'm sorry if we upset you by following you, sir. I only wanted to thank you and shake your hand.'

The man nodded impatiently, as though he already knew all that. Nonetheless, he held out his hand, first to Destiny and then to Anthony.

'The name's Saddler,' he said gruffly.

Before either of them could respond, he continued, 'I've been 'oping for the chance to catch up with you. I need your 'elp.'

Suddenly, Anthony said abruptly, 'Where have we seen you before? I know I recognize you from somewhere.'

'No time for that now. No, no time at all. I'll meet you in the green'ouse. Tonight. Twelve o'clock. I'll explain then.'

And with those words he hurried off leaving the two children staring after him in amazement. They looked at each other again and then burst out laughing.

'The green'ouse?'

'At midnight?'

'Was he for real?' they both gasped together, which made them laugh even more.

'Gosh,' said Anthony, sobering up. 'I wouldn't have followed him if I'd known he was going to turn out to be so weird!'

'We'd better hurry up and get back to our places,' Destiny said, wiping tears from her eyes, 'otherwise Mum's not going to be a happy bunny.'

CHAPTER SIXTEEN

'I can't believe we're actually doing this,' giggled Destiny nervously, as they crept down the stairs in the eerie quiet of the night.

Jenny had not seemed to particularly notice that they'd missed half of the speed stakes and had brushed aside their apologies and explanations of 'getting lost'.

On the way back, they had discussed their strange encounter with the man who called himself 'Saddler'.

'I couldn't smell alcohol or anything,' Destiny said, considering.

'Maybe he's on drugs,' suggested Anthony.

'Yes, but he didn't really seem "spaced out". Just a bit, well you know, peculiar.'

'So what do you think he meant by, 'I'll meet you in the green'ouse, at twelve o'clock? For all he knows you don't even have a green'ouse...er, house!'

Destiny looked at Anthony strangely. 'Well we do, actually. It's hidden behind those trees at the bottom of the garden. But how would *he* know that?'

'Oh, a lucky guess, I should think. Lots of people have greenhouses.'

'Well why did he say he'd been hoping to catch up with us?'

'Dunno, the whole thing is nuts. Anyway, he might guess you'd got a greenhouse, but he couldn't possibly know where you live!'

'Unless –' Destiny rolled her eyes dramatically – 'unless he's following us home, right now!'

Anthony dropped his jaw in mock horror and Destiny giggled. They started taking it in turns to peer around and over their seats to see if Saddler was there, watching them. Some of the other travellers gave them funny looks, which set them both giggling again and earned them warning looks from Jenny to behave.

By the time they got home, everyone was starving again and it was generally agreed that they should order a takeaway Chinese meal. Saddler forgotten, they all chatted animatedly about the show until Jenny yawned, glanced at the clock and announced that she for one was ready for bed.

Once upstairs, Anthony and Destiny discovered that they were not at all tired. That was when Destiny said, 'Why don't we just go and look? You know. In the Green'ouse. At Midnight!'

'You're serious, aren't you,' said Anthony, laughing.

'Go on. Anyway it'll be fun seeing if we can sneak out in the middle of the night!'

'Even if there isn't going to be a crazy man in the greenhouse?'

'Chicken!'

'Am not, just not particularly keen on getting out of my nice snug bed in the middle of the night, on a wild goose...er... chicken chase! Not to mention, your mum is going to kill us if she finds out.'

Destiny grinned. 'She'd better not then.'

They had agreed to wait until both their parents' bedroom lights were out; now Destiny and Anthony were sneaking down the stairs trying desperately to avoid the 'creaky bits'. Finally, they made it to the back door, stifling whispered giggles. The key seemed to make the most enormous clunk as it turned in the lock. Destiny thought it was loud enough to wake the whole street, let alone her mother, but nobody stirred.

Then they were out in the garden. It was very still. It didn't seem like her garden at all, Destiny thought. It looked strange, like some place she had never been before. She shivered; it was quite eerie. As they trod softly down the path, past the shed to the row of trees that hid the back part of the garden, they could see an unexpected glow filtering through the spiky branches. They glanced at each other.

'It can't be,' said Destiny firmly.

Suddenly, they both felt very nervous.

'Maybe we should go back and wake Dad up! I mean, if it's really him, he must have followed us home. That's like being stalked or something!'

As they dithered uncertainly at the edge of the row of trees, the glow moved through the greenhouse towards them.

'It is him, he's coming out!' hissed Destiny frantically. 'Quick, hide!'

But it was too late. Before they had time to move, a figure appeared through the gap in the trees.

'Ah, there you are.' Saddler beamed. 'I was beginning to think you weren't going to come. Not that I'd 'ave been surprised, of course...' he rambled on, chivvying them towards the greenhouse. 'It's not every day a strange man arranges to meet you in the green'ouse, at midnight, I know. You might 'ave thought I was a bit mad like and I wouldn't 'ave blamed you!'

In the greenhouse, he had arranged three crates for them to sit on and another in the middle with a flask, three cups and a plate of biscuits. He chattered on, waving them to sit down. 'I know you young 'uns is always 'ungry and it's a bit nippy, so I thought to myself, I thought, what can you do, Saddler old lad, to make it more cosy for 'em.'

Destiny realized she actually felt both chilled and hungry – two reasons that persuaded her that this wasn't some bizarre sort of dream.

Saddler sat down on his crate. He poured out three steaming mugs of hot chocolate and set to on the biscuits gesturing to the children to do the same.

'Now,' he mumbled through a mouthful of biscuit, 'enough of my rabbit, any questions?'

For a moment or two, there was silence. Both Anthony and Destiny were so amazed to be sitting in the greenhouse, at midnight, with steaming mugs of hot chocolate in front of them, that all they could do was stare helplessly at the man who called himself 'Saddler'.

Then, in a rush, a barrage of questions came tumbling out from both of them at the same time.

'Whoa, whoa.' Saddler held his hands up in front of him, laughing. 'One at a time, please.'

Destiny looked at Anthony and he nodded.

'We want to know why you've been following us and what you meant when you said you've been "trying to catch up with us"?'

'I've been travelling for some time, looking for someone to 'elp us,' Saddler said seriously. 'I've travelled all over your world and I saw something, some months ago now, in a place called Aymerika, which made me very 'opeful.'

'America,' corrected Destiny. 'What do you mean, "your world"?' She glanced at Anthony who raised his eyebrows and shrugged his shoulders.

'Well,' said Saddler carefully, 'I know this is going to sound weird and you're going to think I'm probly just a crazy old man, but...I come from a world called Emajen. There are lots of worlds you see, apart from yours, only not in the same time continuum. There are ways of travelling between 'em, only it's something very few people know 'ow to do...' He trailed off. His face fell and his shoulders slumped at the disbelieving looks on the children's faces. Then his face brightened again.

'There's only one way I can really show you what I mean.' So saying, he picked up a small wooden box from behind the crate he was sitting on. It was beautifully carved with an ornate, black iron lock. Anthony and Destiny looked on curiously as Saddler rummaged in various pockets of his long shabby coat, muttering all the while under his breath, 'I know I put the darn thing somewhere!'

'Aha,' he pronounced, after several minutes of searching. Out of a deep inside pocket he produced a key. It shimmered slightly as though it were alive.

'There you are you little bligh'er. I keep telling you not to be 'opping about in my pockets. You'll get lost.'

Destiny and Anthony burst out laughing, only to be shocked into silence a moment later when a tiny voice shrilled out, 'Much you'd care, you old grump. How do you think it feels being stuck in your smelly old pocket day in day out?'

Destiny creased up. 'That's really clever. Do it again!'

'Oh deary me, you've done it now!' Saddler slapped his forehead rather dramatically and shook his head.

The shrill voice got higher and, if possible, shriller with indignation.

'Ventriloquism! I'll give you ventriloquism! I wouldn't spit out the words that come out of his grimy old mouth!'

Saddler looked at the children appealingly and clapped his free hand tightly over his mouth to prove that the sounds were most definitely not coming from him. The key rattled on until it gradually subsided into an angry mutter. By now it was glowing a dull red colour; the sort of colour people's cheeks go when they are seriously annoyed.

At last Saddler said, 'Look, it's no use you getting on your 'igh 'orse. We got work to do. Now come on and open up the box.'

The key flared redder. 'Not,' it squeaked huffily, 'until they...' here it produced a beautiful silver spark, shaped like an arrow that pointed straight at the children and then disappeared, '... apologize!'

Anthony was the first to recover from his shock. 'We're very sorry,' he said seriously. 'It's just that here we're not used to keys that talk!'

'Well,' huffed the key, 'maybe you just don't listen.' However, it stopped glowing red and began to shimmer again, a pearly kind of silver.

''Ere we go then,' said Saddler, putting the key into the lock of the box. 'You'll 'ave to follow me quick, mind!'

And with that he opened the box and a bright light flooded the greenhouse.

CHAPTER SEVENTEEN

There was no time to pause for thought. Saddler had disappeared through the dark patch that followed the brightness. Without hesitation, Anthony grabbed Destiny's hand and pulled her into the blackness.

For the briefest of moments there was nothing.

The next thing they knew, they were stepping out into a small cottage-like room and there was Saddler beaming all over his face, arms open wide to welcome them in.

'Come in, come in, sit yourselves down. It takes your breath away a bit until you get used to it!'

In fact, both children felt as though they'd been running a marathon and they both gratefully plonked down on the inviting chairs at the scrubbed, wooden kitchen table.

Saddler bustled about putting a kettle on the range. At one point he opened a diamond-leaded window and shouted, 'Mrs Saddler, we've got company.'

To the children, he said, 'I 'spect you're 'ungry. Leastways coming through the gateway always makes me feel starving. Mrs Saddler's prepared a few bits in the 'ope like that you'd agree to pay us a visit.'

Sure enough, the table was laid with a mouth-watering choice of snacks. Biscuits and hot chocolate seemed to have been hours ago, although in truth it could only have been a few minutes. Anthony and Destiny had to admit they both did feel remarkably hungry.

Mrs Saddler came bustling in just as Saddler placed a huge, cheery looking teapot on the table. Mrs Saddler was exactly as they would have imagined her to be in a friendly children's book; small, plump and pretty and just like a female version of Saddler. She came in bringing a fresh outside waft of air with her. In her arms she carried a pot containing several of the largest flowers Destiny had ever seen.

'Mrs Saddler's very fond of 'er garden, ain't you, my dear?'

Mrs Saddler wiped her hands on her apron and somehow managed to fold both children at once in a warm, motherly hug. Turning to Saddler, she queried, 'Milk, Saddler, sugar?'

Left alone for a moment, Destiny whispered to Anthony, 'Is this real, or are we both in the same unbelievable dream?'

Saddler and Mrs Saddler came and sat down at the table.

'Tuck in, tuck in, food first, questions after!'

The children didn't need any prompting.

It seemed easy to talk to the Saddlers about nothing much at all, just as if they were used to visiting a favourite aunt and uncle. Then Destiny said, 'This is all so perfect. It's like, well, it's like everybody's idea of a dream cottage, you know all cosy and sunny and flowery and that.'

'Ah, well,' replied Saddler knowingly, 'where do you think people in your world get their ideas *from*?'

'You keep saying that, *your world*,' said Anthony. 'Where exactly are we?'

'This,' said Saddler, smiling, with some pride in his voice, 'is Emajen. It's not so different to your world really, only we've been 'ere a bit longer.'

'And we don't have talking keys,' said Destiny.

'Mayhap you do,' countered Saddler. 'Only p'raps you don't 'ear 'em! You may think that Emajen seems very poor compared to your world. Your world 'as moved in different ways. You 'ave lots of big buildings and cars and…gadgets, that we on Emajen don't 'ave.'

'You mean technology.' Destiny laughed. 'Like computers and stuff.'

'Ah,' said Saddler, nodding his head. 'Yes, technology, that's the word.'

Anthony looked more serious. 'Why has Emajen turned out to be different, if we're basically the same?'

'Well, we've taken a more…I s'pose you might call it 'mystical' path. Taken more notice of nature, you might say. People in your world 'ave more material things, but they don't take care of their world. And they don't seem very 'appy!'

'But people on Emajen are?'

'Yes! At least they *were*!'

There was a brief silence that hung like a frosty breath and momentarily darkened the bright cheeriness of the Saddlers' kitchen.

It was Anthony who broke the tension. 'What you're saying is, that something has happened here, which is making people unhappy. Something you think we can help with?'

Saddler suddenly looked very weary. 'This may take some time to explain. Per'aps, my dear –' he looked fondly at Mrs Saddler – 'we should 'ave some more tea?'

'Hold on a minute! This is crazy!'

Destiny, who had sat quietly for several minutes, pushed her chair back roughly and stood up, hands on hips. Her eyes blazed and she wagged an accusing finger at a surprised Saddler.

'You must think we're so stupid. I don't know how you've done all this, maybe it's an illusion or…or something you put in the biscuits, but I for one don't believe any of it. Well you've had your fun! Now I want to go back home before our parents discover we're missing and go half crazy with worry!' Destiny glared at the three stunned faces before her and folded her arms firmly.

At last Saddler said sadly, 'Oh dear, I was afraid something like this might 'appen. Of course I'll take you back. Only don't worry, your time moves more slowly than ours. Your parents won't know you're gone!'

He went over to a cupboard and retrieved the box he had carefully stored there.

'Wait a minute!' Anthony looked appealingly at Destiny. 'I have a strong feeling this is real,' he said earnestly. 'At least let's hear why he was looking for us. Then we can go back.'

Destiny heaved a sigh. 'I don't want any trouble, Anthony. You don't know what my mum's like – she'll never let you stay again!'

'There won't be,' he soothed. He looked at Saddler. 'I don't see how *we* can possibly help a whole load of unhappy people in a place we've never even heard of, but you might as well tell us why you brought us here!'

Saddler put the box carefully back in the cupboard. He sat back down.

'I suppose,' he started cautiously, 'that a lot of things we do on Emajen are what you, in your world, might call "magic".'

Here, Destiny shot Anthony an I-told-you-so-this-guy-is-completely-nuts look.

Saddler ignored her and carried on. 'Whereas in your world magic is a sort of "waving your wand around, special power" sort of thing, we don't see it that way. On Emajen, all living things 'ave what we call "mind power". There are people in your world that can use their mind power, but most of 'em have forgotten 'ow. They're too busy with their televisions and their – you know – technology, to use their brains. They think that those who *can* use their mind power, are mad –' here he looked at Destiny – 'or playing clever tricks.'

'But,' said Destiny crossly, 'we *don't* have talking keys. That's like something out of a children's book!'

'Exactly!' Saddler's voice was excited. 'But where do the ideas for those children's books come from?'

'Well, people's imagination, of course!'

'And what's imagination when it comes down to it?'

Destiny shrugged. 'I don't know,' she snapped impatiently. 'I'm not a psychologist!'

'Ah.' Saddler looked triumphant. 'It's memory. Memory from a long, long time ago, when 'uman beings were aware of these things. Things they've long since forgotten 'ow to 'ear or see.'

'Even if what you say is true, I still don't see what all this has to do with us.'

Mrs Saddler smiled warmly and got up to refill the teapot.

Destiny looked at Anthony searchingly. 'You're not really buying all this stuff, are you?'

'A lot of people don't really believe the stuff we do with the horses,' he replied. 'I'd just like to know what Saddler thinks we can help with!'

Saddler looked at Destiny, then Anthony, then back to Destiny again. His face was a big question mark.

Destiny deflated. 'I s'pose.' She sighed. 'But if Mum finds out we're gone, you can do all the explaining!'

Saddler looked relieved. 'I'll tell it as briefly as I can. A long, long time ago, at the very beginning of all time, our two worlds were not so very different. There was water and land and sky and tiny things that lived in the water. Over time, they evolved and some of 'em came out of the water and learnt to exist on the land. Eventually, some of 'em found out 'ow to conquer the skies. I believe that's pretty much 'ow things 'appened with your world too.'

'How do you know so much about our world though?' asked Anthony.

'Ah, well, I 'appen to 'ave a very good friend 'oo came 'ere from your world. One of the very few what knows 'ow to travel between 'em. 'E's called the Prof and I 'ope that you'll soon get the chance to meet 'im. Anyway, this is where things get interesting. Why it is that two very similar worlds can produce so many different creatures, I dunno. We 'ave "quaves" – I believe you call 'em "cats" and we 'ave "harets" – think that's "dogs" in your world. Oh and we 'ave "nators", which I know you'd be glad of seeing as 'ow you're obviously very fond of 'orses the pair of you. Although most of ours can talk of course!' Here Saddler grinned at Destiny. She gave him a rueful smile and he continued.

'Some of your creatures seem very strange to me. The Prof took me to see a...oh now, what did 'e call it...big grey thing, wrinkles, long nose...'

'Elephant!' cried Destiny and Anthony together, beginning to catch his enthusiasm.

"Oh yes. El-e-phant,' Saddler repeated carefully. 'Very strange. And...' he patted his arm, '...arm, arma... armadillo – funny, snuffly thing, with what looks like slates on its back! And...well, anyway –' he caught himself in mid flow – 'anyway, you see what I mean. The point is the Prof tells me that people in your world are finding new, wonderful creatures all the time. And that others are believed to exist, but 'ide 'emselves away.'

'Like the Yeti,' said Destiny excitedly, her interest, as always, roused by the subject of animals.

'As you say.' Muttering to himself, Saddler rummaged in one of his many pockets and produced a stub of pencil. From another came a tatty folded up piece of paper. On it he wrote 'YETI', in large capitals. 'Mmm,' he said, having forgotten the children for a moment, 'I must ask the Prof about that one!' Looking up, he saw the children watching him quizzically.

'Oh, erm...where was I...oh yes. As in your world, Emajen relies on a balance of things, to keep everything ticking over smoothly. We 'ave one animal what is very, very important to us. They 'ave a greater mind power than any other creature on Emajen. They're beautiful, proud and kindly creatures and it's their goodness and positivity that protects Emajen from 'arm. They 'elp to make it the 'appy, wonderful place it is!'

'What do they look like?' asked Destiny, enthralled despite herself.

'They're a cross between a nator and a quave – that's why they're called "Natorqua".'

The children were surprised to see Saddlers eyes fill with tears.

'Such beautiful, beautiful animals and now someone,

something, is poisoning their minds. Destroying them one by one, so that the very thread of Emajen's existence is being unravelled!' Saddler covered his eyes with his hands.

'There, there don't fret, my dear,' Mrs Saddler comforted, patting his hand with her own.

At length Saddler looked up, wiped his eyes with his sleeve and gave Mrs Saddler a watery smile.

'That's why Emajen needs your 'elp!' he said at last.

Destiny and Anthony looked at each other puzzled. They were in no doubt at all now that Saddler was telling them the complete truth, but how could they possibly help?

Destiny got up and put her hand on Saddler's arm. 'I'm sorry I didn't believe you,' she said gently, 'but I really don't understand what you think we can do!'

Saddler had composed himself and smiled up at her gratefully. 'We've been silly,' he said sadly. 'I can see that now. The Natorqua 'ave always been there. We've always taken it for granted that they were…that they always would be. Now that something is 'appening to 'em, no one in Emajen knows what to do or 'ow to reach 'em.'

'What exactly *is* happening to the Natorqua?' Anthony frowned.

'Slowly, but surely, their minds are being poisoned. They're becoming aggressive and their anger is beginning to spread throughout Emajen. Gone are the days when anyone could wander freely among 'em, breathing in their calm and beauty. Now no one can go near 'em. At first they just ran away, but lately they've been threatening to attack anyone what goes anywhere near. That's if you can find 'em. They've gone into 'iding, just like your Yeti!

It was the Prof 'oo suggested I should look to your world for 'elp. 'E said I would find someone there, 'e was sure, 'oo would know about the workings of animal minds. Animals like the Natorqua. Someone 'oo might be able to undo the damage before it was too late.'

'But why us? Why not a grown up. Surely you need an animal psychologist or something!'

'An animal psychologist 'oo would even believe Emajen existed?' Saddler looked hard at Destiny, who felt herself blush. 'And if they did believe it, what then? 'oardes of people from your world coming into Emajen and bringing their technology? No, we want to look after Emajen, not destroy it!'

'Good point,' said Anthony. 'Although not all our technology is bad.'

'But you still haven't explained why us!' persisted Destiny.

'Because my travels took me to a place called Ay...America and there I saw two young people what seemed to 'ave an extraordinary affinity with animals. That poor dog was so grateful that you came along. Another minute or two and that paw would 'ave been seriously damaged!'

Destiny's mouth gaped.

'And as for you, young man, seldom 'ave I seen such gentle 'andling of nators...I mean 'orses, ever.'

'You were at the ranch?' Destiny's eyes looked as though they might pop out with amazement.

'Just passing through,' said Saddler airily.

'I *knew* I recognized you from somewhere.' Anthony grinned. 'You look a bit different without the sunglasses and lairy shirt!'

CHAPTER EIGHTEEN

For a short while there was silence. It seemed to Destiny that Anthony had quite happily accepted everything that was going on. She still couldn't quite get her head around it all. She glanced up at the window. Outside, the shadows were lengthening. Could someone really make you hallucinate a whole new place, with objects that talked and sunshine that softened towards the end of the day; just like it might do on any day? When they had left the greenhouse, it had been about half past midnight. It was December. Cold, with days that seemed to end almost before they'd begun. Yet here they were on a warm, late autumn evening. What had happened when they followed Saddler through the blackness?

Saddler caught Destiny's glance. He seemed to follow her thoughts.

'Hmm, about time we were getting you home then,' said Saddler, getting up and reaching for the box once more.

'It's been a real pleasure.' Mrs Saddler beamed, hugging the two children for the umpteenth time. 'I do 'ope you'll come and visit us again soon!'

This time Anthony and Destiny were ready for the bright light followed by the dark blob and all three stepped through the darkness together.

It seemed so incredibly peculiar to be back in the greenhouse. It was still dark outside and a white blanket of frost had covered everything in their absence. Destiny shivered and thought longingly of her warm, toasty bed.

'So what happens now?' asked Anthony, pointedly.

'Well, it's a long journey to where we think the Natorqua are... or at least where they were last seen. It's a lot to ask, I know!'

'How far is it?'

'Ahh, it might take a few days.'

'But that's impossible,' cried Destiny. 'Even if we could help you, there's no way we could be gone for a few days. Time isn't that much slower on Earth!'

'No, no, not ordinarily, no. But there may be a way. Could we meet again? Tomorrow night? And I'll explain.'

By now, Destiny was so tired, she would have agreed to almost anything to get back to bed. Anthony looked as though he felt much the same.

'Great.' Saddler beamed. 'Tomorrow then.' And he disappeared in a flash of brilliance.

The house was as dark and silent as when they had left it a few hours before. They didn't have the energy for nervous giggling as they stole back up the stairs. Back in their rooms, they were both were asleep almost before their heads hit their pillows.

CHAPTER NINETEEN

Jenny and Matt both chuckled when Destiny and Anthony finally appeared, bleary-eyed, for a very late breakfast the next morning.

'Kids today, they've got no stamina!' Matt laughed.

Having spent a day at the stables where Destiny now shared a pony, they made excuses early in the evening to go up to Destiny's room and excitedly made plans for the night ahead. Destiny shivered with anticipation. 'I still can't quite believe it's all real,' she said.

It felt even less real as they crept once more down the creaky staircase and out into the chill of the night.

'Maybe we just had the same crazy dream last night,' whispered Destiny as they neared the greenhouse.

'I don't think so,' replied Anthony. 'Dreams are usually muddly. Last night was certainly strange, but it didn't jump crazily from one thing to another like dreams usually do! Anyway, look...' He pointed to the familiar glow coming from the greenhouse.

There were no crates or mugs of hot chocolate this time. Saddler greeted them warmly, but said, 'We need to 'urry. We got things to do today.'

So saying, he pushed the key firmly into the box and, before they knew it, they were standing once more in his bright, cosy kitchen. Mrs Saddler was there to give them a welcoming hug and a bar of chocolate each to munch on the way.

'On the way where?' queried Destiny.

'I'll explain as we go,' said Saddler.

It was a beautiful autumn morning with only the odd wisp of fluffy cloud trailing across an otherwise clear, blue sky. Saddler said 'morning' to a bird perched on the fence post, but it stopped singing abruptly and flew away.

'Hmph!' growled Saddler. 'See what I mean? It comes to something when the birds are too scared to even pass the time of day!'

'You said you would explain where we were going,' said Anthony, to take Saddler's mind off the bird.

'Ah yes, well now. We're going to see someone. 'Er name is Nebiré. She's probably the wisest person on Emajen. She can use eight-nine per cent of 'er mind-power, so they say. She'll be able to 'elp us!'

'If that's true, how come she can't use her mind-power to help the Natorqua?' asked Destiny.

Saddler shook his head. 'The Natorqua 'ave lost their trust in other beings from this world. And their collective mind-power is much stronger than Nebiré's. Besides, she would never make the journey – you'll see!'

For a while they walked on in silence, each one wrapped up in their own thoughts. The sun was rising towards noon. It was pleasantly warm and the sounds of bird song wafted through the balmy air. Destiny found that, if she listened very closely, the songs did in fact have words. They didn't make a lot of sense until she realized that the birds were singing to each other, or rather talking to each other in little sing-songy voices. She smiled to herself, maybe that's where the 'chattering of birds' comes from, she thought.

At that moment the smile disappeared from her face as she experienced a sharp stinging pain in her ankle.

'Ow!' she yelped. Looking down she saw that there was blood trickling through her sock and onto her trainer. Anthony and Saddler had both spun round to look at her.

'Are you all right?'

'I think something bit me.'

Saddler scoured the ground. 'Aha,' he crowed and swooped down on something not far from where Destiny was standing. When he stood up he had what looked like a small, furry ping-pong ball pinched between his finger and thumb.

'What's *that*?' asked Destiny, rubbing her ankle.

'That,' said Saddler disgustedly, 'is a Grund. Nasty little blighters!'

The children looked closer. Huge, innocent eyes blinked at them out of the soft, round fluff.

'Are you sure it bit me? It looks so cute!' Destiny stretched out her hand to stroke the soft fur.

'Watch out!' yelled Saddler.

The creature's eyes disappeared as a huge gaping mouth sprang open to reveal a full set of sharp, vicious-looking teeth. Destiny's eyes bulged with horror. She snatched her hand away just in time, as the fangs slashed together, missing her fingertips by a whisker. The Grund wriggled furiously in Saddler's grasp and started hurling abuse at them in a gruff growl that seemed incredible coming from such a small, sweet-looking creature.

Saddler glared at it with disgust. 'Only one thing you can do with these. You might not want to watch!' he said apologetically. So saying, he dropped the Grund on the floor and raised his leg in the air. Destiny flung her hands over her eyes, but that didn't cut out the rather unpleasant squelching sound Saddler's boot made as it came back down again, hard!

Anthony put a restraining hand on her shoulder, knowing her well enough by now to know what might happen next. But Destiny was too shocked to be angry.

'I can't believe you just did that!' she said quietly, and then hurried off up the road to hide the tears that sprang to her eyes.

'I'm sorry!' Saddler looked really woebegone. 'Never seen one of 'em 'til about a few months back. Now they're everywhere. Once they get 'old of you, they very often don't let go. Still, we'd better be getting on.' He looked around cautiously. 'Where there's one, there's bound to be more!'

So saying, he hurried off after Destiny. Anthony frowned, shook his head and then strode after them.

Nothing else untoward happened and within about an hour they reached a densely wooded area at the top of a small hill. Here Saddler plunged out of the warm sunlight into the cool shade of the trees. Occasionally, a ray of sunshine managed to filter through the leaves but then it would disappear as though made to feel unwelcome by the thick gloom. It was strangely silent: no rustling in the undergrowth, no bird song, nothing. Even Saddler, who had soon regained his natural bubbliness after the Grund incident, muttered, 'Stick to the path,' and then fell silent.

The path was narrow and wound like an unruly ribbon between the trees. At one point, Destiny looked back, but the way behind them seemed to have been gobbled up by the murk. She could almost have thought that the trees had moved together obscuring the path completely. Except of course she knew that couldn't happen!

It seemed to take an age to wend their way through the wood and they were beginning to wonder if, in fact, they were lost, when the path ended abruptly and they stepped out into a bright, sunlit glade. The glade swelled at the far end into a small hill: a hill with a door in the centre and a chimney from which wisps of bluish-grey smoke curled. As they watched, the smoke formed various shadowy shapes, which then fizzled away into the clear blue sky. They gazed for a moment, fascinated. The outline of a bird appeared. It flapped its wings once and then faded. Then a rabbit wiggled its ears, took a gigantic leap and was gone into the blue yonder.

A stirring from within the hill broke the spell. The door creaked open and a vast shape loomed in the doorway.

CHAPTER TWENTY

How to describe Nebiré? She was grotesque and beautiful at the same time. The shape that lumbered through the opening could have been no more than five feet tall, but made up in girth what it lacked in height. As Nebiré stood surveying the group, they could see a kind of sparkling aura that shimmered around her from top to bottom. Her face was heart shaped, accentuated by the way her hair parted in the middle and fell, long and straight almost to the ground. A single eye regarded them with brilliant, purple intensity. She was stunningly beautiful, despite the three chins that wobbled beneath her delicate jaw. Two of her hands rested on the huge, wide hips; the other two gestured to the group to follow. As she shuffled round, large webbed toes appeared beneath the flowing gown she wore. The children were so stunned, that they couldn't say anything, but Saddler had regained his cheeriness and shouted out, 'Morning Nebiré,' in a hearty voice. Nebiré lumbered back through the doorway. As she shambled, her hair parted slightly. Destiny stifled a gasp. A second eye, as startlingly blue as the other was purple, gazed out at them from beneath the strands. It crinkled upwards slightly at the corners, as though it had heard the gasp and was smiling. Then the hair swung across again and it was gone.

Nebiré led them, walking painfully slowly, her breath rasping harshly with every step, up a dimly lit passage. Other passages branched off here and there, but they took no twists or turns and suddenly the passage opened into a wide room. It was much bigger than you would have thought from the outside and a large picture window filled the room with light. Crystals hung from the ceiling, which tinkled and spun in a light breeze. Every so often a shaft of sunlight would catch one and send a rainbow of colours skittering about the room. Saddler, who had obviously been here before, made straight for the hearth and picked up the kettle that was quietly simmering there. Nebiré oozed her bulk into a great, padded wicker chair and motioned the children to sit nearby on piles of big, soft, brightly coloured cushions.

'You know that path of yours gets worse!' Saddler chuckled, as he placed a tray of drinks on the table next to Nebiré's chair. 'I thought we were never going to get here.'

Nebiré laughed. It was a deep, rumbling sound that seemed to come from somewhere far down inside her.

'It keeps unwanted visitors away,' she replied in an equally deep, rasping voice. 'And it occasionally likes to have a little fun with friends!'

'Now.' The beautiful smile vanished and her face became serious. She looked at Anthony and Destiny who were sitting rather awe-struck on the floor next to her. 'I have heard a lot about you from my friend here. Also my crystal web shows me many things.' Both right arms waved at a group of crystals hanging at one end of the room. Now that they looked closer, Anthony and Destiny could see that the pattern they made did in fact look like a spider's web.

'You want to know why I cannot reassure the Natorqua?' continued Nebiré. 'We all have our own skills. Mine lie in seeing the past, the present and what in time may well come to be. But you, between you, possess the mind-power to reach all living creatures. More than you realize. Much more. If you use that power wisely, in time it will grow, become stronger. But for us, here on Emajen, there is not much time. We can only hope that the powers you possess now will be strong enough!'

Anthony looked straight at the one, piercing purple eye.

'I...' he glanced at Destiny, '...we, don't understand what it is you think we can do.'

'It is our hope that you will agree to journey to where the Natorqua have concealed themselves. The crystals have followed their trail so far, although I cannot always clearly see them.'

'I can't understand,' said Destiny. 'Why anyone would want

to poison them!'

'For centuries we have lived at peace in our world. The Natorqua have kept it so. But there is evil abroad. It has come from another place. I am getting closer and soon I will know from where, but for now I am still in the dark.'

'Supposing we found the Natorqua, I can't see what we could do!' said Anthony.

'The crystals may be able to tell us – we shall see!'

Nebiré used all four hands to heave her bulk out of the chair. She shuffled across the room to where the crystal web shimmered and glittered. She began working the crystals with long sensitive fingers turning and weaving them. The room became very still. To begin with, hundreds of rainbow colours flickered around the room, but as they watched a bright, white light began to glow in the centre of the web. It spread from one crystal to the next, round and round in circles until the whole web was suffused by its brilliant glimmer. All the while, Nebiré muttered and weaved. Finally, she stopped. The light began to fade to be gradually replaced by a picture.

Destiny and Anthony gasped. Clearly visible in the distance were two figures walking up a stony path. It didn't take long for them to realize that they were seeing themselves. The figures walked towards them, gradually moving into clearer focus. They looked tired and dirty. They were saying something to each other, although their words couldn't be heard. They seemed to agree on something and the Destiny in the picture flung down a rucksack and sat down heavily on a big rock at the side of the path. Anthony squatted beside her. He looked as though maybe he was explaining something. He scooped up some stones into a pile and then spread them with his hands. The onlookers could see the stones trembling and one or two rolled a little. Anthony seemed to watch them carefully. He pointed to one and then looked at Destiny, as if asking her opinion. Destiny nodded and Anthony grabbed up the stone, weighing it thoughtfully in his hand. The picture faded.

Everybody shook themselves as though they had just awoken from a deep sleep.

'So,' said Nebiré gruffly, 'the crystals have spoken!'

'But what does it mean?' Anthony and Destiny asked simultaneously.

'You will know – when the time comes!'

* * *

The path back was completely straight and walking along it took about half the time it had previously.

'You will know – when the time comes!' intoned Destiny in a gruff, mysterious voice. Anthony laughed. Walking through the fields in the late afternoon sun, they felt as though some kind of weight had been lifted from their shoulders.

'You shouldn't make fun!' chastised Saddler.

'I'm sorry, it's just I thought you said she would give us some answers. "You will know – when the time comes" wasn't exactly helpful!'

'Let's hope we will,' said Anthony thoughtfully. 'Still, at least we have this...' he lifted a small box and looked at it reflectively, '...which has solved one of our problems!'

The box Nebiré had given them held a small phial containing a few drops of a bitter, yellow-coloured liquid. After Nebiré's comment, there had been a long space of silence, each of them lost in their own thoughts. Then at last, Destiny had said, 'I don't see how we can help. It could take days, maybe weeks to even find the Natorqua let alone work out what to do about them. I know time moves slower here, but not that much slower. We can't just disappear for that long!'

Nebiré, once more settled in her chair, had put the tips of her fingers together and closed her eye. She stayed that way for so long they thought she had fallen asleep. Then a low hum rippled from her throat, her eye sprang open and she stretched out one hand, staring intently at a table across the room. The table was covered with hundreds of different bottles and phials of all shapes and sizes. They watched amazed as the bottles all jiggled and rattled animatedly before settling again to an expectant stillness. Slowly, smoothly, a small bulb-shaped phial had risen above the others and floated across the room. It landed gently on the palm of Nebiré's outstretched hand and seemed to nestle there contentedly like some small animal. Nebiré had bent close to her hand and muttered over the phial for some moments. At last she had straightened; a radiant smile lighting up her face.

The phial, it turned out, contained a substance so strong that it would, for a short time only, freeze time on Earth. It was the only way Nebiré could give Anthony and Destiny the time they needed if they were to help find the Natorqua.

'I hope it will give us long enough!' Destiny and Anthony had both exclaimed at the same time.

In spite of the seriousness of the situation, Destiny had giggled. 'We keep doing that – saying the same thing at the same time, I mean!'

Nebiré had merely raised her graceful eyebrow and said nothing.

So they now had the means to buy some time. There was, however, a snag. The potion would only work if they could persuade another human being to drink it. They had each had a sniff and turned their noses up in disgust. Apparently it tasted worse than it smelt.

'No chance of slipping it in someone's tea then!' Anthony had grimaced.

Back once more in Destiny's bedroom, they stored the phial safely on the top shelf of her wardrobe, along with the other thing Nebiré had given them. It was a very small egg timer. She had told them to turn it once as soon as they had administered the potion; that way they would know roughly how long they'd got before their time ran out. They were too exhausted to discuss what they were going to do about the potion and decided to think about it the following morning. With a sigh of relief, Anthony finally said, 'Goodnight,' and disappeared into his room next door.

CHAPTER TWENTY-ONE

For the next couple of days, Anthony and Destiny racked their brains trying to think how they were going to get someone to swallow the foul smelling, evil-tasting potion. They mooched around getting under Jenny's feet and driving her to distraction. Then two nights after they had last seen Saddler, they were awoken by the sound of stones hitting Destiny's bedroom window. Blearily, she opened it and peered down into the darkness below. Anthony's sleepy face emerged from the adjacent window seconds later.

'What is it?' whispered Destiny.

At first Anthony couldn't see anything, but as his eyes became accustomed to the dark, he just made out a shadowy figure standing on the patio below.

'It's Saddler! Come on, he's going back down to the greenhouse.'

Destiny groaned. The thought of leaving the comfort of her warm snugly bed to go out in the freezing cold was not appealing.

'Must we?' she hissed

'I think it must be important, or he wouldn't have risked coming this close to the house.' Anthony's head vanished.

Destiny sighed and rooted about for her trainers under her bed.

When they reached the end row of trees, they could see the light Saddler always carried bobbing backwards and forwards as he paced up and down the length of the greenhouse.

'Oh, thank goodness.' Saddler smiled, but it was a shadow of his usual cheerful beam. 'You two are 'ard to wake.'

'Could be something to do with not having had much sleep for two nights,' muttered Destiny.

'Ssh,' said Anthony, frowning at her. 'What's up, Saddler?'

''ave you found a way to, you know, give someone that there

potion?' asked Saddler hopefully.

'Not yet. It's hard. We've come up with all sorts of ideas, but nothing we think would work,' said Anthony.

'Problem is, see, things are getting very much worse. Nebiré 'as seen a strange purple shadow in the north, not far from where she thinks the Natorqua are. It's spreading. And people are beginning not to trust each other. And I had to step on five Grunds this morning, just to get down my front path!' He looked at Destiny apologetically. 'I 'ate to nag,' he said worriedly, 'but I think something needs doing sooner rather than later!'

'We know.' Anthony looked perplexed. 'But we just can't think how to give it to anybody. If it didn't taste and smell so bad...'

There was a silence.

'I've got it!' yelled Destiny excitedly, making both Anthony and Saddler jump. 'I've got the perfect solution – doh, why didn't I think of it before?'

Anthony and Saddler looked at her expectantly.

'Granddad's coming tomorrow,' she continued in a rush. 'He's always falling asleep – and he snores, with his mouth open!'

'That's it then,' grinned Anthony, catching her enthusiasm. 'We'll wait until he's snoring and drop it in. Easy!'

Destiny loved her granddad and was always very pleased to see him, but even he was delighted and rather surprised by how warm her welcome was when he arrived.

Their opportunity arose not long after lunch. It was Sunday and a large roast dinner was guaranteed to work its magic. Sure enough, he was soon comfortably seated in a chair in the lounge and within minutes his eyes began to close.

'This is it!' whispered Anthony as they both ran lightly up the stairs to fetch the phial and egg timer from their hiding place. By the time they got back downstairs however, Matt had seated himself on the sofa and was reading a book.

'Hi, you two, what are you up to?'

Granddad grunted, but thankfully didn't wake up.

'Erm, we...er...just thought we'd go on the computer, didn't we, Destiny...if that's okay?'

'Fine by me, only keep the noise down, I might have forty winks myself in a bit.'

'Let's hope he falls asleep before Granddad wakes up!' breathed Destiny.

For what seemed like hours, they kept on glancing surreptitiously at Matt who showed no signs at all of drifting off. Destiny was getting quite absorbed in a game of solitaire when Anthony nudged her. Looking round cautiously, she saw that Matt had put his book down and closed his eyes. They played on for a few minutes to be sure that he had really fallen asleep. Granddad was snoring gently, head back, mouth open.

'Thank goodness he's not snoring loudly,' said Anthony. 'At least he won't wake Dad up.'

'We'd better be quick.' Destiny could feel every muscle in her stomach clenching with the fear that one of the two men would wake up and catch them out. Anthony undid the lid of the phial so that he would be ready just to tip the few drops of liquid straight into Granddad's mouth. They had discussed who should do the deed the night before. Destiny had said that she was sure her hands would shake too much, whereas Anthony was used to being calm in difficult situations.

Now Destiny put her head around the lounge door just to check that her mum was nowhere about. She gave Anthony the thumbs up. They padded silently across the carpet, Destiny desperately trying to control a nervous giggle that seemed to have lodged threateningly in the back of her throat. They stood looking down at her granddad sleeping peacefully.

'Here goes,' whispered Anthony. He positioned the phial so that it was only a couple of millimetres away from Granddad's mouth. He gave one quick glance at Destiny and then tipped up the phial.

The liquid was quite thick and seemed to take forever to slide down the glass.

One drop

Two…

The last drop was just hanging by the slightest gossamer like thread, waiting to fall into the abyss below, when Granddad gave an almighty snort. In that briefest of moments before the final drop fell, Destiny and Anthony looked with horror, first at each other and then at Matt, who had started up violently at the sound. Wrenched out of a deep slumber, his confused mind was confronted with the vision of Anthony and Destiny slightly stooped over her granddad, whilst Anthony poured something bright yellow into the old man's mouth.

'What the devil…' But there was no time to finish the words.

The last drop fell.

There was silence.

Complete silence.

Destiny slowly let go of Anthony's hand, which she had been clutching tightly. Nebiré had warned them not to touch anyone else as they administered the potion, otherwise that person would also remain outside the time freeze.

'The egg timer,' whispered Destiny hoarsely, still afraid that Matt might easily be woken once again. Neither man stirred however. Anthony turned the timer and then tucked it firmly into his pocket.

'Come on,' he said urgently. 'We have to get back to Saddler's, there's no time to waste.'

'Sorry, Granddad,' said Destiny sorrowfully, as she gazed down at the half-awake look of shock and disgust on his face. Planting a kiss on his forehead, she grabbed her jacket and rushed after Anthony.

CHAPTER TWENTY-TWO

When they arrived at the greenhouse, Anthony immediately made for the place amongst various discarded pots where Saddler had told them the box would be hidden. Glancing at Destiny, he took a deep breath before plunging the key into the keyhole. Without Saddler to go before them, it seemed a much scarier thing to do than it had before. The next thing they knew however, they were standing in Saddler's kitchen once more. The warm afternoon sun filtered lazily through the windows and everything was quiet.

'I hope that potion really works,' said Destiny, 'otherwise we're in big trouble!'

'I've no doubt it will! More importantly, what do we do now?' said Anthony, putting the box and the key carefully down on the table.

At that moment, a beautiful, sleek black and white cat leapt lithely through the open kitchen window and landed soundlessly on the wooden table. It had four white paws and a rather fine white moustache, which instantly sent Destiny into exclamations of delight.

'Oh, how beautiful!' she crooned. She stretched out her hand to tickle him under the chin.

'The last time you did that, you nearly got your hand bitten off!' Anthony laughed.

The cat gave him a withering look.

'I am *not* a Grund!' it retorted in a silky voice. Then turning to Destiny it purred, 'Thank you for the compliment. I have been told –' a quick lick to the paw – 'that I am quite handsome. Ahh yes, you may scratch there a little more, my dear.'

Anthony raised his eyebrows and Destiny, restraining the urge to giggle, dutifully scratched behind the cat's ears a little more. At last, shaking its head and arching its back in a curving stretch, the cat sat down and looked at them both solemnly.

'Saddler is at a meeting with the Prof. He asked me to see if you had arrived yet and, if so, to tell you that he won't be very long. Please feel free to make yourselves at home. As you see, Mrs Saddler has left some cakes on the table in case you're hungry. A pleasure to meet you.' So saying, the cat sprang lightly onto the window ledge and, with a flick of his tail, disappeared into the garden.

They didn't have long to wait before Saddler appeared. It was growing dusky and his lantern brought with it a cheery glow.

'Ahh, there you are.' He sounded relieved. 'I was 'oping you'd make it. I've just been chatting to the Prof. First thing tomorrow morning, that's where we'll go. 'E and 'is lad 'ave been 'unting out all sorts of provisions for us to take.'

Saddler seemed more cheerful again, now that they were actually preparing to do something.

The following morning, the children were roused by the most wonderful breakfast smells. Mrs Saddler was determined to give them a hearty send off and neither of them needed to be asked twice to tuck in. Mrs Saddler's cooking was exceptionally tasty!

Saddler appeared very soon after they had sat down, having already been out to fetch a paper. He smiled at them all and bade Anthony and Destiny a cheery good morning, but his eyes held a worried look.

'Not good news again, my dear,' he said gruffly. 'Not good at all.' The front of the newspaper had a large picture of a Natorqua lying curled up on the ground. It was obviously dead.

'EMAJEN'S LIFE-BLOOD SEEPS AWAY'

read the heading. Underneath, a subheading stated, 'LOCAL MAN TERRORIZED BY GRUNDS'.

The story told how these small, innocent looking creatures

were now attacking in packs and how the poor old gentleman in question had been obliged to fight them off with his walking stick. It was only due to Nebiré's help that he had very quickly been able to re-grow the toe that one of the Grund's had viciously bitten off!

Saddler looked first at Mrs Saddler and then earnestly at Anthony and Destiny.

'I'm beginning to wonder if I've done the right thing in asking you to come 'ere. I 'ad 'oped we might be able to get to the Natorqua before things got too bad.' He sat down at the table and put his head in his hands, unable to keep all his worry to himself any longer.

'Of course you've done the right thing,' said Destiny. 'We'll figure out something.'

Saddler lifted his head and shook it slowly from side to side.

'I'm just afraid it's going to be too dangerous, my dear. There must be some other way.'

'I think we've probably done the worst bit –' Anthony laughed, attempting to lighten Saddler's mood – 'trying to get that wretched stuff down Granddad's throat. You should have seen the look on Dad's face!'

Destiny laughed too. Then she looked seriously at Saddler.

'We're here now, so it looks as though you're stuck with us. Besides, time's getting on, so we'd better get going!'

Looking from one to the other, Saddler finally stood up and squared his shoulders. There was an expression of mixed pride and gratitude on his face. If Anthony and Destiny could be so determined, then what on Emajen did he have a right to whinge about?

'Right then. Let's go!'

CHAPTER TWENTY-THREE

The day was a gem. The morning sparkled, a perfect example of a clear, crisp autumn day. Small, white cotton wool clouds did their stuff, almost competing with each other to make the most fascinating shapes. Birds trilled, sang and chattered. Two dear little rabbits hopped out of the long grass on one side of the track. They put their little paws up to their noses at the sight of the three travellers, giggled audibly and hopped out of sight again.

'Oh,' breathed Destiny, 'how adorable!'

It was, apparently, about a two-hour walk to the Prof's place and, as the morning wore on, the day became brighter and warmer and altogether more perfect.

'It seems impossible to believe that there's anything at all wrong here,' said Anthony. 'Everything's so calm and peaceful!"

'Well let's 'ope it stays that way!' remarked Saddler.

A tall, imposing house stood at the end of a short path that was guarded by soaring, majestic looking trees.

'What's that?' said Destiny, tilting her head to catch an almost inaudible hum that reverberated gently through the air.

'I can hear it too,' said Anthony, intrigued.

Saddler smiled. 'It's the trees snoring. They're nocturnal you know, really, trees. They come awake mostly when it's cool and dark. That's why you wouldn't want to be walking through Nebiré's wood too late in the day!'

Destiny laughed delightedly and then guiltily clamped her hand across her mouth.

'It's all right,' chuckled Saddler, 'they won't 'ear you. Sleep through anything, trees will!' He patted the trunk of the nearest tree and turned to walk up the path. A long delicate twig swayed gently as if tickled by the breeze; it caught the tip of Saddler's cap and snagged it off his head.

'Oy!' roared Saddler. 'None o' that now!' He jumped up furiously in an effort to retrieve his cap, but it remained just a hair's breadth too high. Anthony and Destiny howled at the spectacle until tears poured down their cheeks. Shooting them a look of disgust, Saddler gave up on his cap and stomped away up the path. Anthony looked at the tree with awe.

'That was so cool!' He laughed. 'I guess maybe we should give Saddler his cap back now though!'

Destiny watched fascinated as the twig lowered just enough for Anthony to recover the cap. He thanked the tree politely and its leaves rustled as if in acknowledgement. Somehow, without having a face, the tree seemed to smile. It was a sort of upwards lift of its bark, but Destiny knew she was right, it was definitely a smile.

The Prof appeared in the doorway of the house, hair fuzzing everywhere, and beamed broadly at them all.

'Welcome, welcome,' he said, and ushered them in.

Anthony grinned at Saddler and handed him back his cap.

The Prof's house was a treasure trove. There was mess everywhere. Well, not exactly mess, more a generally organized chaos. The Prof waved a hand airily at some chairs and instructed the group to clear themselves a seat each. A vast mahogany desk groaned under the weight of books, files and papers and an assortment of intriguing looking gadgets.

'Been inventing anything today, Prof?' enquired Saddler, as he deftly removed a pile of manuscripts from an easy chair and placed them carefully on the floor.

'As always, as always.' The Prof beamed. 'Here's a little idea I had in the wee, small hours.' He picked up a small round object the size of a ping-pong ball. It was a purplish-grey colour and it looked remarkably like a Grund. Destiny stiffened. However, on closer inspection, the object was clearly covered in tiny spikes rather than fur.

'What does it do?' she asked.

'I call it a Grund Buster and the idea is it acts as a decoy. I've made a pretend Grund to try it out on. I was just about to test it out, when you arrived.'

'No time like the present,' said Saddler.

The Prof needed no further encouragement. He placed the Grund Buster on the floor and tapped it gently with his foot. It emitted a low growl that sounded almost exactly like a Grund.

'The idea is that any nearby Grunds will be attracted to the sound.' So saying, he placed his pretend Grund on the floor near to the decoy. 'Then when the real Grund gets near enough, our Grund Buster squirts it with a sticky fluid that immobilizes it for long enough for the Grund Buster to then finish the Grund off with its spikes.'

'Gross!' said Destiny

The Prof pushed the pretend Grund nearer to the decoy with his toe. Sure enough, a stream of sticky liquid shot out from the decoy, missed the pretend Grund by several feet and squirted half way up the Prof's trouser leg. The decoy then gave a low growl and rolled off in completely the opposite direction.

'Oh well, it needs some adjusting,' said the Prof sadly, as he dabbed at his trouser leg with a hanky.

'Great idea, though,' said Anthony, impressed.

'Well now –' the Prof ran his hands through his unruly mop of hair – 'my inventions are all very well, but that's not what you came for. We have lot of preparations to make.'

'That's right,' said Saddler, gazing with some revulsion at the Prof's sticky trouser leg. He shook his head as though to clear his mind and looked earnestly at Destiny and Anthony.

'You're sure now…'

'We're sure!'

'Enough said then. By Nebiré's latest reckoning, the Natorqua are only a few days journey away and we'll 'ave Kaz to 'elp us.'

'Kaz?' queried Destiny.

'He's a horse.' The Prof smiled. 'He says he doesn't mind

pulling a cart just this once, as it's all in a good cause.'

For the umpteenth time Destiny and Anthony glanced at each other. It really was hard to get their heads around animals that actually talked.

'Probably moan the 'ole way!' grumbled Saddler.

The short silence that followed was broken by the appearance of a small boy, with thin almost elfin features and dark hair that contrasted starkly with his pale complexion. He slipped in silently and stood close to the Prof's side, gazing at the other three with wide, enquiring eyes.

'Ah, Squib!' The Prof gazed down affectionately at the boy and put an arm protectively about his shoulders.

Squib, it turned out, had been very busy. There were three rucksacks neatly laid out in the kitchen with all sorts of useful items stowed away and enough provisions for a couple of days. Hopefully they would need no more than one stop along the way to re-stock.

'How long do you think the potion will last?' Destiny said anxiously to Anthony.

Anthony dug deep into his jacket pocket and took out the tiny egg timer. He peered at it closely. A few grains of what looked like pale, rainbow-coloured sand speckled one end, while the other was nearly full.

'How do we know it hasn't just tipped back into the full side?' said Anthony.

The Prof beamed. 'Actually, it's one of my more successful inventions,' he said modestly. 'A one way egg timer. Nebiré says she doesn't know how she ever managed without it. Try it and see.'

Destiny pulled a slightly disbelieving face, as the decoy Grund flashed through her mind. Anthony gingerly turned the egg timer upside-down. The sprinkling of grains that had peppered the bottom slid, as if pulled by a magnet, towards the timer's concave centre. Destiny held her breath. If the Prof's invention didn't work, they would have no way at all of knowing how much time had passed and, more importantly, how much time there was left.

Destiny glanced up and saw Squib watching her. He smiled and nodded his head encouragingly. By now Anthony had turned the egg timer completely upside-down. It was difficult to tell – because there had only been a small number of grains in the bottom to begin with and because the egg timer was really tiny – whether it had worked or not.

'Now turn it back the other way,' enthused the Prof.

Anthony did as instructed. Sure enough, a few grains only plummeted down from the middle of the timer to lie still and pale at its base.

'Cool,' said Anthony. 'How long since we gave your granddad the potion, our time I mean?' he asked Destiny.

She looked at her watch and wrinkled her nose. 'About twenty hours I think.'

'Hmm, well we've only used up a few grains, so I guess that means we've got plenty of time left!'

'Nonetheless,' said the Prof, 'we don't know how easy it will be for you to locate the Natorqua, or how long you may need when you do!'

There was a silence as everyone digested this comment. Then the Prof rubbed his hands and said cheerily, 'Right, lunch, I think. Then we have a lot to plan and discuss and preferably a prompt start in the morning.'

CHAPTER TWENTY-FOUR

Saddler and the Prof had talked on late into the night, pouring over a rather ancient-looking map and discussing the merits of various routes and detours, none of which meant a great deal to Anthony and Destiny. At some point, Destiny had dozed off in a big comfy chair by the open fire, which crackled away merrily. She vaguely remembered following Squib and Anthony up several flights of stairs and sinking into the most deliciously soft bed. The next thing she knew, it was morning again and tantalising breakfast smells were wafting up the stairs.

They set off in good spirits, sitting on blankets in an old but sturdy looking wooden cart. It was another beautiful day. They waved at the Prof as Kaz plodded away, Squib sitting pixie style on Kaz's broad back. They could still hear the Prof shouting various last minute reminders and injunctions to 'take care', when they were well out of sight. When they couldn't hear the Prof any more, Squib came out of his shell and began to chatter nineteen to the dozen, as though between them he and the Prof could weave a web of protection around the travellers. He told them all about how he had met the Prof and, proudly, how he had learnt to read and write and was now learning all about the planets and the stars. After a while though he fell silent and without warning slipped from Kaz's back and was gone.

'Funny little chap,' Kaz murmured fondly. He pulled a tasty looking morsel from the hedgerow with his teeth and munched it lazily as he clopped along.

The day wore on. They stopped for lunch when the sun seemed to be at its highest point in the sky. Destiny had given up looking at her watch. It was confusing when the sun showed roughly one time and her watch showed something completely different. It wasn't even as though you could reset it like when you went abroad. The time just moved differently here. After about the hundredth time of glancing at her wrist, she gave an exclamation of annoyance and crossly undid the strap, shoving the offending object into her rucksack.

It was mid-afternoon when they reached a crossroad. Kaz came to a halt and contentedly munched on some grass by the side of the track. Saddler stretched and reached for his rucksack.

'Can't quite remember what we decided was the best way 'ere.' So saying, he pulled out a small scroll of parchment.

Out of nowhere there came a distant rumble of thunder. It grew rapidly louder. The ground beneath them began to shake. A violent wind whipped up around them and the cart began to shudder. The sky, now darkened by an immense black cloud, seemed to press down on them like a huge oppressive hand.

It was at this point that Kaz bolted. Saddler was flung violently backwards, lost his balance and toppled off the back of the cart, just managing to grab hold of the side as he did so.

'Saddler!' screamed Destiny and Anthony, their voices lost beneath the deafening rumble and the howling of the wind.

Anthony grabbed Saddler's arm and both children strained to draw Saddler back up into the thundering cart. At last, Saddler scrambled to safety, doggedly clutching the map in one hand. Anthony turned to see to Kaz, when he heard Saddler give a furious yell. As he spun around, a vicious gust of wind tore the map from Saddler's grasp and it disappeared up into the thunderous cloud just as though someone had sucked it up through a giant straw.

For a brief second, Destiny could swear she saw a beautiful face with a cruel smile amongst the dark clouds. Then it was gone. Everything stopped. Kaz came to an abrupt standstill and everyone sat in still, silent shock.

Saddler was the first to pull himself together.

'Everyone all right?' he asked shakily.

They nodded dumbly. Anthony climbed stiffly out of the cart and approached Kaz who stood panting, head hanging.

'Kaz? Are you okay?'

The poor horse was trembling. He shook his head dejectedly from side to side.

'I'm sorry,' he mumbled.

'What for?' Anthony ran an expert hand over Kaz's back and legs, checking for any signs of injury.

'I'm no good!' moaned Kaz. 'I'm useless. I'm a useless nator. I ran away. I might as well be quave food!'

'We were all terrified,' soothed Anthony, satisfied at last that Kaz was, at least physically, okay. Kaz lifted his head and his ears perked up.

'Really?'

'Really!'

Destiny came up and put her arms round Kaz's neck. She squeezed him affectionately.

'You are *so* cute,' she murmured, 'and you sound just like Eeyore! And I'm sure your quick thinking saved us from a whole load more trouble!'

'I am? I do? It did?'

Obviously Kaz thought that sounding like 'Eeyore' must be high praise indeed. His chest swelled and he blew Destiny a gentle puff down his nose. Anthony grinned and rolled his eyes, but everyone suddenly felt a whole lot better.

Saddler stoked up a small fire and made them all tea. Tea, he said, was a brilliant Earth invention. It didn't taste quite the same on Emajen – different leaves, but it was just as nice – kind of nutty and Saddler believed you couldn't ever have enough tea!

'Well,' said Saddler at last as he packed the tea things back in his rucksack, 'we've lost the map, so it seems sensible to me to keep going until we get to the next signpost. Then we'll see if we can find a place to 'ole up for the night.'

All agreed, they set off once more and Kaz had decidedly more spring in his step, but Destiny was quiet and thoughtful.

She hadn't mentioned what she'd seen, or thought she'd seen, to the others; it sounded too daft!

'Do you often have freak storms like that here?' she asked Saddler at last.

Saddler scratched his head. 'First one I've ever seen, but then a lot of things 'ave been 'appening round 'ere what's not normal!'

'Oh!' Destiny shivered. The memory of that cruel smile made her blood run cold.

As they continued on their way, the day clouded over once more. It began to rain, not hard, but a persistent drizzle that clung in wet beads to everything it came in contact with. By the time they reached the next junction, the rain had begun to fall harder. They were wet, lost and miserable. Kaz had lost the spring in his step again and his head was drooping once more.

'Well at least we'll 'ave somewhere to aim for,' said Saddler, trying to lighten the situation. But the junction only offered a left or right turn and the sign post – when they eventually found it – had fallen over and was lying in the bushes.

'Great!' said Destiny. 'What do we do now?'

CHAPTER TWENTY-FIVE

By the time they had stopped dithering and made up their minds which way to go, it was getting dark. Kaz plodded along miserably, muttering about his aching feet and the fact that the road seemed to have turned into a rutted track.

They were beginning to think they would have to spend the night out in the middle of nowhere, when Anthony spotted a light in the distance.

The darkness had descended very quickly, the sky as starless and cheerless as the scene below it. It took about another hour for the bedraggled bunch to reach the source of the light. What they found cheered them immensely. It turned out to be an inn as cheerful and friendly looking to their weary eyes as the night behind them was gloomy.

Inside, the innkeeper welcomed them heartily. Destiny felt like she was living a scene from some tale of 'Ye Olde England' and she remembered what Saddler had said about where people on Earth had got many of their ideas from.

They sat at a round table in a snug little corner, by the side of a roaring fire. Outside the rain spattered against the windows, no longer threatening now that they were safe and warm and rapidly drying off inside the bustling inn.

The innkeeper was a small, round, jolly fellow, who rubbed his hands together a great deal and seemed to have a permanent beaming smile fixed on his face. He bustled over to their table and drew the curtains across the window behind them with an expansive gesture.

'Never known anything like it!' He chortled.

Anthony checked on Kaz, making sure that he was comfortably stabled and had plenty of hay to munch, whilst Saddler ordered them some food and secured them a couple of rooms for the night.

'Now, we need to decide what we're going to do in the morning, since we've no idea where we are!' said Saddler through a satisfying mouthful of rather delicious pie.

'Do you think the innkeeper might have a map we could buy?' asked Anthony.

'Or at least might know where we could get one,' suggested Destiny.

The next time the barman appeared to collect their dishes, Saddler raised his query, but the barman greeted the question with a perplexed furrowing of his brow.

'Well now, people around these parts aren't generally in need of maps. I don't know as I can help you there.' He rubbed his chin thoughtfully and was just about to make a suggestion when a small, dark-haired man from the next table got up and hurried over to them.

He bowed politely and smiled. Destiny shivered. For some reason, she didn't like the smile; it somehow didn't quite reach his eyes.

The man introduced himself and said, 'I accidentally overheard your conversation. I do hope you don't think it rude of me to interrupt, but I gather you wanted a map.'

His voice was nasally and rather whining. Destiny glanced at Anthony, but he was concentrating on the man and she couldn't read his expression.

'It just so happens,' continued the man, 'that I too am a stranger around these parts and I have various maps about my person. Whereabouts are you heading?'

The innkeeper, Destiny noticed, had actually lost his smile and was looking at the man with clear dislike. She willed Saddler not to be too specific, but to her relief when he spoke he just said, 'Me and my friends 'ere are just exploring the area.' He spoke politely, but Destiny could hear the suspicion in his voice and she breathed a sigh of relief.

The man returned to his table and came back with an

assortment of maps. The innkeeper wandered off, muttering something inaudible under his breath, but his wide smile had resurfaced by the time he reached the bar.

Saddler looked at the maps closely and at length tapped one with his index finger.

'This should do us nicely, if you can spare it – 'ow much do I owe you?' He dug in his pocket looking for his coin bag.

'No, no! I wouldn't dream of it. More than happy to help out a fellow traveller.' The man smiled creepily and Destiny had to quickly repress a shudder.

'That's most decent of you, but then allow me to buy you drink with our thanks. It's the least I can do to thank you for your kindness!' Saddler stood up and put a friendly arm around the man's shoulders, steering him towards the bar.

Destiny cringed at the very thought of having to even touch the man and when she glanced across at Anthony she could see that the expression etched on his face exactly mirrored her reaction. With the stranger gone, however her mood lifted and she laughed.

'Your face! It's a good thing he's got his back to you!'

But although he smiled, there was a thoughtful look behind Anthony's eyes.

'I think we should take turns at keeping watch tonight!' was all he said.

CHAPTER TWENTY-SIX

Their rooms were small but pleasant, with oak beams, wonky floors and in Anthony and Destiny's room two, comfy four-poster beds. There wasn't room for anything else apart from a solid old chest of drawers but, as Saddler said, they weren't planning on staying long.

It was late by the time they trudged up the creaky wooden staircase. The inn had slowly emptied as they re-lived their experiences of that day, unable to make head or tail of what had happened.

Saddler wished them a weary good night and then disappeared into his room.

Destiny flung herself down on the nearest bed. Her head was spinning with weariness and she had to force her eyes to stay open.

Anthony looked as shattered as she felt, but he stood resolutely by the window and said, 'I'll keep first watch. We'll do two hours each, turn and turn about, okay?'

'Okay.' The word slurred between Destiny's lips as she sank immediately into a death-like stupor.

It seemed only minutes later that Anthony was shaking her awake. Groggily she sat up on the bed, rubbing her eyes; her mouth sandpaper dry. Glancing around, she could see two glasses on the chest of drawers but no water. She decided to have a quick look outside for a bathroom.

Feeling her way carefully to try to avoid any loud, creaky bits, she opened the door softly and peered out into the corridor. A single, dim light lit the way to a 'rest room', mercifully only a few doors down.

A couple of minutes later, having slaked her thirst and feeling considerably better, Destiny wandered back down the corridor. As she approached the bedroom, she frowned a little, sure that she had pulled the door to behind her. Thinking that Anthony might have woken and wondered where she was, she hurried forward, opening her mouth to reassure him. What met her eyes however caused more of a strangled gurgle to emanate from her vocal chords.

A figure was bending over Anthony's bed and its stance was distinctly menacing. At the sound of Destiny's approach, the figure turned with an evil leer, saliva drooling from its lips. Destiny found her voice and screamed as loudly as her lungs would allow. Instantly, Anthony shot up and they both watched in horror as the intruder's grin stretched and widened and his whole face began to swell. In front of their eyes the creature's grin completely disappeared as a grotesque, slavering jaw shot forward. Its eyes shrivelled to piercing pinpoints in its monstrously bloated head and the skull shrank into huge, fleshy shoulders. It had the appearance of some hideous, hairless wolf-bear and, as sabre like talons sprang from its engorged fingertips, it snarled and twisted once more in Anthony's direction.

Anthony had slid off the bed and was desperately looking round for something to defend himself with as Saddler came crashing through the doorway. The creature swung around once more just as Saddler lunged, brandishing a large iron poker. He caught the beast a glancing blow on the shoulder and it roared with pain. It swiped a vast, distorted fist at Saddler, knocking the poker clean out of his hand and sending him sprawling. Saddler hit the fireplace and slid down the wall where he lay, quite still.

Anthony and Destiny stared at each other aghast, but now the enraged creature advanced towards Destiny. Grabbing for the remaining glass, Anthony threw it as hard as he could, knowing he could only hope to distract the brute for a moment. Totally beside itself now, the creature spun and lunged for Anthony. Destiny needed no second chance. With strength born of fear and desperation, she made a grab for the poker and swept it up, her terror for Anthony overriding everything.

'Hit the base of its skull – the base...' screamed Anthony. The creature leered over him dripping fetid spittle on his face and making him gag.

Destiny lifted the poker high. She brought it down with a crashing blow right on the very base of the monstrous beast's skull. The result was electric. And stunning. The creature didn't even groan; it just slid to the floor with a satisfying thud. Stone dead!

Destiny's arms shook from the effort. Saddler had regained consciousness just in time to hear Anthony's yell and watch the blow fall. With a look of mingled horror and relief, he grabbed them both and pulled them roughly back into the doorway. He ventured back into the room and peered at the prostrate body. Contrary to most horror stories, it hadn't reverted to human form – he could only assume then that this was its natural state.

'It's dead all right!' he said.

'Thanks, Destiny, I owe you one!' said Anthony shakily.

'I think we owe each other! How did you know that stuff about the base of the skull?'

'I just suddenly remembered we had an osteopath staying at the ranch one time. Somebody asked him how you could kill someone with one blow and he said, "Hit them in the Occipital Atlantal Joint, old fellow!" I've never forgotten it!'

'Just as well!' remarked Saddler. 'Doesn't it strike you as a bit odd that no one 'ere seems to 'ave 'eard anything. I think we must 'ave made quite a racket!'

'Maybe no one else is staying,' said Destiny.

'Hmm, you'd think the innkeeper would 'ave 'eard something though! Anyway, I think it's 'igh time we got out of 'ere. There's something mighty strange going on and I'm not sure I want to wait and find out what!'

Destiny hurriedly gathered their things together, while Anthony tried to wash off the sticky spittle that still clung to his face and hair. They tiptoed through the silent building and were just hitching Kaz up to the wagon when Destiny gasped and clapped her hand to her mouth.

'Forgotten something,' she gabbled, and before they could stop her, she had plunged back into the inn.

CHAPTER TWENTY-SEVEN

The group were sombre as they plodded through the grey drizzle of the early morning. Even Destiny's quick thinking in retrieving the map had only briefly lifted their spirits. In their hurry to leave, the map had been left on Saddler's chest of drawers. Destiny had been brave. Not only had she gone past the room where the creature lay, but had also had the courage to glance in on her way past.

To her utter horror, the body had gone! As she told the others, it was as if the room hadn't even been used.

Now she said, 'Maybe the blow only stunned it?'

'Nah, it was most definitely dead,' said Saddler.

'And if it was dead, then that means someone knew about it and cleared up all the evidence!' said Anthony.

'Well it's lucky they only had one body to clear up then, and not three!' Destiny said pointedly. It didn't help to lighten their mood any.

Nobody felt much like talking and it was a sad, bedraggled group that rattled forlornly onwards. At one point they stopped for a mug of tea and a snack even though no one really wanted to eat. Even Kaz picked morosely at the grassy verge, just to show willing.

They plodded on. Saddler mechanically muttered instructions to Kaz each time they came to a junction or a crossroads and then relapsed again into his own thoughts.

Suddenly, Anthony sat up straight.

'I don't know if it's just me, but I'm sure I recognize this spot! And has it occurred to anyone that every time we've come to a turning we've gone left!'

'So,' grumbled Destiny. It had been drizzling constantly and she felt as though an entire cloudful of rain had trickled right down her neck and seeped through her skin to the bones beneath.

'Well,' said Anthony, with exaggerated patience, 'if you keep turning left and left and left, where are you going to end up?'

'Back where you started,' groaned Saddler, suddenly awoken from his reverie.

Destiny grabbed the map from Saddler's hands.

'This isn't a map at all, it's...it's a stupid fake!'

She glared angrily at the paper. To her consternation, the roads and landmarks began to swirl like miniature leaves caught in a sharp gust of wind. She watched with horror as they formed a face. A familiar face. A beautiful face, with a mouth that twisted into a cruel smile. Her chest tightened. Gasping for breath, she flung the map over the side of the cart and watched in dismay as it burst into flames.

Immediately, Anthony was at her side. He put his arm round her shoulders in an effort to calm her shaking.

'What was it? What did you see?'

Trembling, Destiny told them about the face she had seen in the clouds.

'I thought it must be my imagination,' she stammered through chattering teeth.

'And you saw the same face just now on the map!' said Saddler.

It was more of a statement than a question. Destiny nodded glumly.

With the grim realisation that, yet again, they were hopelessly lost, the group decided their only course of action was to keep going until they found somewhere that they could rest for the night. But as time went on and the shadows lengthened, it became increasingly obvious that there was little if no habitation to be found.

Saddler attempted to be positive. 'We'll 'ead for those 'ills over there. At the very least, there's some clumps of trees that'll give us some shelter.'

Kaz did his best to help too. He lifted his head and picked up his pace, so that they trundled along at a brisk walk.

Destiny however was disconsolate. She couldn't believe they'd been so easily duped. Before too long, they reached the foot of the hills and the shelter of some trees. Destiny had muttered herself into an exhausted doze, so Anthony and Saddler left her in Kaz's capable hooves and went to search for possible shelter.

A brief sojourn brought them about halfway up the nearest slope, which opened out onto a kind of natural, rocky path. Not far along the path were a series of openings in the side of the hill, any of which would provide suitable shelter for a night. They located one with a slight overhang that looked as though it would protect them from the rain and then wended their way back down the hillside to the cart. They found Destiny awake and chatting to Kaz, while she fed him apple treats from a bag.

The clouds had begun to break up, allowing a surprisingly bright, late sun to push out comforting tendrils of warmth. The water can was bubbling away merrily on the small camping stove and the whole scene cheered Anthony and Saddler tremendously.

The sun began to dip slowly towards the horizon as they finished their impromptu picnic. Discussion had taken place in a much more positive frame of mind and decisions had been reached. They knew the rough direction they should be travelling in, even if the map had gone, so it was agreed that they would spend the night in the cave that Saddler and Anthony had found and then set off again at first light, northwards; something Saddler's compass would take care of.

Kaz, complete with cart, could obviously not be expected to make it through the narrow trees and up the rocky hillside. It was agreed, therefore, that the travellers would only take the most important items of equipment with them and that Kaz, minus cart, would make his way post haste back to the Prof. It should be no problem to enlist the services of one of the larger birds to bring them another copy of the map.

Only Destiny was uncertain. The thought of sending Kaz back alone filled her with concern. She fussed over him, stroking his nose and asking him repeatedly if he was sure he would be okay. Kaz, loving every minute of such lavish attention, gracefully accepted the titbits she bestowed on him and blew softly down his nose at her.

'Just as well nators can't be sick!' Saddler remarked, half amused and half irritated.

Finally they persuaded Destiny to let Kaz go. It was definitely getting dark and they wanted to make sure they could find their way back to the cave. Destiny had to be content with one last, lingering kiss on his nose before Kaz trotted off into the dimming light.

The rain, which had abated briefly, began to fall more heavily again just as they were approaching the entrance to the cave. A small fire and a few candles later, and the cave had taken on quite a homely air. They had brought candles at the Prof's suggestion to save on torch batteries, and their welcome glow helped to radiate a little warmth, as well as dispelling some of the darker shadows.

They made themselves comfortable and settled down to sleep. Although the rain pounded down endlessly outside, inside they were snug and warm. Even Destiny's bones seemed to have dried out! They left just a couple of candles burning, knowing that it was wise to preserve supplies.

It seemed no more than a few minutes later that Destiny was awoken by something. The candles, burnt down to small stubs showed that she must have been asleep for a few hours.

Unsure what had woken her Destiny lay still, listening intently. Nothing. The cave was silent apart from Saddler's gentle snores. She was just slipping into a drowsy slumber once more when a noise jerked her rudely awake again.

The noise, a kind of rustling or scratching, came from the back of the cave. Destiny shifted around in her sleeping bag and strained to pierce the shadows in the dark recesses.

Her movement alerted Anthony, who had been disturbed by the same noise.

'Did you hear it too?' he whispered.

Destiny jumped.

'Sorry!'

Destiny could almost hear him grinning in the darkness.

'What do you think it is?' she breathed, not wanting to wake Saddler.

They both slipped noiselessly out of their sleeping bags and picked up a candle each. Cautiously they advanced into the thick, viscous blackness towards the rear of the cave.

CHAPTER TWENTY-EIGHT

The cave stretched further back than they had at first anticipated. They moved carefully, anxious not to disturb anything that might have made its home there. Stopping every few steps, they moved their candles around cautiously; searching for signs of whatever it was that had caused the strange scratching sounds.

After a couple of minutes they reached the back of the cave. There was nothing. Just a solid wall of rock and no signs of anything, animal or otherwise, that might have been making noises there. They looked at each other puzzled.

'Maybe whatever it was heard us coming and ran away,' whispered Destiny.

'I'm sure we'd have seen or heard something!'

The candles were on the verge of sputtering out, so they turned to retrace their steps.

The noise occurred again.

They both spun around so sharply that the candle flames were immediately snuffed out.

'Damn!' they both exclaimed at the same time.

It was then that Destiny noticed something odd. As her eyes became accustomed to the darkness, she could see just the tiniest sliver of light filtering through from somewhere at the back of the cave.

She touched Anthony's arm and pointed to it. What they hadn't seen, couldn't see by the light of the candles, was that the cave in fact had two backs, the right side overlapping the left. The difference between them was only very slight, creating a gap just big enough for a person to squeeze through. The glow of light was more obvious close to and, by peering through the opening, they could see that the gap widened almost immediately into a reasonable sized passage, that ran straight for a few paces and then bent away sharply to the left.

Destiny went to wriggle through, but Anthony held her back.

'I'll go and get Saddler,' he said firmly.

'But...'

'Think about it. There've been some pretty peculiar things happening just lately. How do we know this isn't just another attempt to stop us finding the Natorqua?'

The vision of a cruel face flashed into Destiny's mind. She shuddered.

'Look, I'll go on my own. We don't want to risk two of us stumbling around in the dark. I'll be as quick as I can!'

'Don't be too long!' hissed Destiny after Anthony's dimly retreating figure.

It can have been no more than three or four minutes later that Destiny heard the sound of approaching footsteps and muted voices, though to her, waiting, it had seemed like an age. Relief flooded through her, only to be immediately extinguished by the fear that maybe it wasn't them at all. Maybe there had been something waiting when Anthony got back. Something horrible. Maybe it had already silenced Saddler and then Anthony. Maybe now it, or even they, was coming for her! She clapped a hand over her mouth, resisting the urge to scream. Slipping through the cave wall, she hid behind the overlapping rock, heart pounding so loud she was certain anyone within a mile's radius would hear it.

'Destiny?' the familiar whisper sent a deep sigh of relief shuddering right through her. She slipped back through the gap and flung herself thankfully at a surprised Saddler.

'Whoa, you're okay, it's okay,' he soothed, patting her on the back in a fatherly fashion that instantly reassured her.

'Sorry!' she muttered.

'Nothing to worry about! Now what 'ave you two been up to this time!'

CHAPTER TWENTY-NINE

Having established that Saddler was just about able to squeeze through the slit in the cave wall, the group decided that they would retrace their steps, pack up their things and explore the passage further.

In a way, as Saddler suggested, it might be to their advantage. Possibly, disappearing underground for a short spell might throw whom or whatever it was off their trail.

Anthony slid through the opening first to retrieve the belongings that Destiny and Saddler passed through. Destiny followed and turned away to suppress a giggle as Saddler sucked in his breath and grunted and wriggled and squeezed his way through. He emerged on the other side with an almost audible 'pop', as though the rock had become fed up with him and finally spat him out.

Saddler dusted himself down and gave Destiny a disgruntled look that told her plainly she still had the trace of a smile on her face. Then he led the way. With silent footfalls, they crept towards the bend in the passage. Saddler peered around it and motioned the others to follow. To their amazement, the passage was now lit at regular intervals by hanging lanterns.

'Someone's been 'ere recently,' whispered Saddler. 'Look, these ones 'aven't long been lit!'

'Maybe that's what the scraping sound was,' said Destiny. 'They're quite high. Maybe someone had to bring a stool or a ladder or something and dragged it on the ground?'

'You could be right. What we don't know is whether that somebody is friend or foe. We'd better be on our guard!'

The passage continued for some way before disappearing around another bend. At varying intervals on either side, other tunnels could be seen meandering off into the distance. One or two were also lit by lanterns. Most were not.

The passage they were in led gently, but steadily downwards. When they reached the bend, Saddler motioned the other two to hang back while he peered cautiously around the corner.

He snapped his head back so quickly, Destiny was amazed it didn't give him whiplash.

With a finger to his lips, Saddler beckoned them forwards. What they saw took their breath away. It was a cavern which must, virtually, have been as high as the hill itself. It was vast. All around the curved walls, lanterns burned. The light from these was reflected in myriad prisms, which had been cleverly placed high up on the walls and around the ceiling itself, parrying the reflected light from one to the other. The effect was stunning and the whole chamber was lit as though it were a glade on a bright, sunny day.

Thankfully, the cavern was empty, save for a raised platform at the far end on which stood a long table and some chairs.

'What do we do?' whispered Destiny, who suddenly felt very nervous about leaving the relative safety of the dim passage. Once they stepped into the cavern, there was nowhere to hide if someone came along.

'I think we should go back,' said Anthony, but looking at Saddler's radiant face something told him this was probably not an option.

It came as rather a surprise when Saddler turned and led them back up the passageway. He ducked into the first unlit offshoot, flicking on his torch as he did so, and followed the beam until they came to a small alcove. Here, there were several small boulders resting against the walls, as though they might have been deliberately put there for people to sit on.

With a sigh, Saddler plumped himself down and his face took on a dreamy, faraway kind of look. Anthony and Destiny sat down next to him and Anthony shone his torch at Saddler to jolt him out of his daydream.

'What's going on? Did you know about this place?'

'No, no.' Saddler immediately looked chastened. 'I mean, I did know *of* it, at least I'd 'eard that it existed, but I didn't know precisely where...and then what with the passages and the great chamber and all...'

'What?' Destiny and Anthony both clapped their hands over their mouths at the same time realising that, in their frustration, they had both yelled out.

Anthony continued more quietly, 'What are you talking about? You're not making any sense!'

'Sorry, sorry, no I'm not am I?' Saddler visibly pulled himself together and began to explain.

'You know by now that there are other worlds in existence apart from your own. And you also know that it's possible to travel between 'em if you 'ave the know 'ow. It's not something that too many people know about, which is just as well.'

'Why's that?' asked Destiny

'Well, the Prof told me all about the wars in your world and 'ow different countries 'ave invaded each other throughout 'istory. Imagine the chaos it would cause if you 'ad several worlds vying for supremacy over each other!'

'That's true.'

'Anyway getting back to the point, worlds only have a certain length of life; they live a long time, but not forever. New worlds are being born all the time. Your world is pretty old and your keeper, so Nebiré tells me, is getting a bit weary with all the devastation 'umans keep causing.'

'Our keeper?'

'Yeah, you know...uh what d'you call 'er. I read it only the other day...'

'You mean Mother Nature?' asked Anthony

'Exactly that! Mother Nature. What your world needs now is a few more in'abitants like yourselves. A bit more Earth-friendly like. Give your keeper a bit of a 'and, take the strain off so to speak.

Anyway, some while back, the Prof told me about some creatures called 'Creations' 'oo come from a very strange place.'

'Creations?'

'Yeah. You won't believe this, Destiny you're good at art right? Well, 'ave you ever doodled, you know created odd sort of cartoon creatures?'

'Yes of course, but...'

'Well you can bet your boots that they're alive!'

There was a stunned silence while the children digested this bizarre piece of information. Then, in the dim torchlight Destiny grinned broadly.

'Oh very funny. You really had me going there...' But the smile faltered on her lips at the expression on Saddler's face.

'You're not kidding, are you?'

'NO!' boomed a harsh voice from behind them. 'He's not!'

CHAPTER THIRTY

Anthony, Destiny and Saddler all jumped around to see a most peculiar creature standing at the entrance to the alcove. Two beady eyes glared at them from above what could only be described as a trumpet like protuberance. The creature's small, rotund body ended in two, largish three-toed feet.

'This is private territory and you are trespassing!' the creature boomed crossly. Destiny found herself once more having to smother a giggle, as she noticed a colourful mop of feathers flopping about agitatedly on top of the creature's head.

It waggled three tentacle-like arms in their direction and barked an order that Destiny couldn't quite catch.

In no time at all, they were surrounded by creatures of all shapes and sizes, some so incredible that Destiny thought she must be having some kind of fantastic daydream. But she only had to look at the others' faces to know, if this was a dream, they were all dreaming the same thing.

They were marched (hopped, bounced and slithered) back down the torch-lit passage until they stood in the vast cavern once more. Several more creatures sat at the table on the platform, seemingly deep in discussion. After a few moments, one of them stood up and came hurrying over.

'There is much to discuss. The prisoners are to be taken to the "secure room", while we decide their fate!'

So saying, he turned on his hoof and hurried back to the table.

The children and Saddler were led down more torch-lit passages until they came to a sturdy, wooden door. The door was evidently very heavy because a large creature with huge hairy arms and an elephant's trunk stepped forwards and heaved it open with all his strength. The group were ushered inside and the door closed quietly behind them.

On their own once more, the three travellers looked at each

other stunned.

At last Anthony found his voice.

'What on earth just happened there?' he said, shaking his head in wonder.

'Well, for a start I think we were very slow off the mark,' mused Saddler. 'I 'ave a feeling if we'd said "boo" loudly enough they'd 'ave all run away!'

Destiny exhaled a long, slow breath.

'They were *amazing*,' she breathed. 'Did you see the one with the hair that looked like strings of pearls and...' she set off on an excited monologue about the various incredible characteristics she had seen. She was so absorbed that she didn't notice the heavy door opening once again, until a gentle cough startled her in mid flow.

A small face beamed at her. A face she knew very well indeed. Destiny swallowed and felt her cheeks flush.

Saddler and Anthony both looked at Destiny. They looked at the creature and back at Destiny. Anthony grinned.

'It's not, is it?'

'Well I didn't know, did I?'

Turning her back on the creature, she hissed in Saddler's ear, 'They don't know do they? I mean, who actually drew them or... or whatever?'

'I'm not really sure, but I don't know 'ow they could. The Prof never mentioned that.'

Plastering a smile on her face, Destiny turned slowly around until she was facing the creature, which was waiting expectantly.

'Hi!' she said.

'Hi,' repeated the little fellow in a voice that sounded eerily like her own. His little, triangle mouth widened into a cheeky grin.

'I'm Boff. Pleased to make your acquaintance!'

'Boff! That figures!' Anthony smiled broadly at Destiny and then gazed wonderingly at the sizeable, complex brain that pulsed and glowed through Boff's translucent skull.

'Nice...er...nice shorts,' Saddler said with a remarkably straight face.

Small light bulbs flashed on and off around Boff's head as he digested this comment. Finally, he grinned his triangular grin again.

'Thanks,' he said, smoothing the tartan material with one hand. 'I'm very proud of them!'

Destiny groaned. 'I was only seven!' she muttered.

'To what do we owe the pleasure, Mr Boff?' asked Saddler.

'Oh, just Boff. I mean not Just Boff, just Boff!'

'Okay not, Not Just Boff, to what do we owe the pleasure?'

Light bulbs flashed.

'Saddler!' scolded Destiny.

But at that moment Boff laughed. It was an appealing, infectious sort of laugh, so like Destiny's that Anthony was prompted to remark, 'Scary!'

'A good joke.' Boff laughed. 'We're a bit rusty on jokes down here.'

He went on to explain that he had been appointed as their personal 'comforter', which meant that, whatever they needed during their stay, he Boff would do his level best to acquire it for them.

'Can we back track a bit there?' said Saddler. 'When you say "our stay", what exactly does that mean?'

'Ah, well, you see you've caused a bit of a flap down here,' said Boff. 'As you've probably guessed, we don't often have visitors from above; at least, not unexpected ones. The council of Eldons are meeting to decide what has to be done.'

'And how long might that take?'

'Oh, a day or two, I shouldn't wonder. The Eldons will come up with several options and then of course we all have to vote for the option we think best and then—'

'Listen,' interrupted Saddler, 'I need to talk to someone in charge, right now! It's really important! We can't afford to delay!'

Boff blinked his eyes uncertainly. He looked worriedly at Destiny as though for encouragement. She smiled warmly at him and nodded.

'We really, really do need you to help us, Boff,' she said.

This seemed to reassure him and in a flash he had knocked on the door and disappeared through it as soon as it opened.

'Whoa! What are the odds of *that* happening?' said Anthony.

'What d'you mean?'

'Well you drew him, didn't you?' I mean it's pretty far fetched for people's doodles to be coming alive somewhere to start with, but what are the odds of meeting one…let alone one you actually drew!' Anthony laughed. 'By the way, what possessed you with the shorts?'

But Destiny was spared answering by the return of Boff with an Eldon.

The Eldon appeared to have a more or less human body with a donkey's head. Destiny was fascinated by his eyes. They were huge and soft and framed by the longest, curliest lashes she had ever seen. She realized she was staring and quickly looked away. The Eldon sat gracefully on a boulder.

'Boff here tells me you have some urgent information for the council. I agreed to come because he is widely respected among us for his sound judgement!'

Boff's brain matter flushed a delicate rose colour.

Saddler wasted no time in telling the Eldon about what was happening on Emajen and why it was so important that he and the others be allowed to continue with their journey. The Eldon nodded from time to time, but passed no comment. When Saddler had finished, the expression on the Eldon's face was grave.

'If what you say is true – and even down here we have noticed certain stirrings of unrest – this is serious indeed! I will relay everything you have told me to the council. I can't promise to speed up the proceedings, but I will do my best to impress on them that time is of the essence. In the meantime I will leave you in Boff's capable hands.'

So saying and with a graceful incline of the head, the Eldon was gone.

It was impossible to tell how much time had passed since they had first found the opening at the back of the cave. They all realized however that they were feeling quite hungry. Boff hurried away to find them food and returned laden with goodies. He was about to leave them to eat, when Destiny touched his arm.

'Boff, since we have time to kill, why don't you stay a while. There's far too much here just for us!'

Boff looked closely at Destiny and realized that, for some unaccountable reason, he totally trusted her. A couple of his bulbs flashed.

'That would be nice, thank you.'

CHAPTER THIRTY-ONE

They chatted idly for a while. Boff was full of questions about where the children came from. The light bulbs on his head flashed so enthusiastically that Destiny became quite anxious in case he got over excited and the light bulbs exploded. Noticing her increasingly alarmed expression, Anthony gave her a calming smile and turned to Boff.

How about you, Boff? How do you and your...um...'

'Fellow Creations...'

'Yeah, Fellow Creations... How do you come to be here?'

'Ah, it's a long story,' Boff said, shaking his head sadly. His brain wobbled slightly from side to side as if in agreement.

Destiny found herself feeling very protective of Boff and it hit her almost like a physical pain to see the sad look on his face.

'Poor Boff,' she cried. 'You don't have to tell us if you don't want to!'

'I bet it's a fascinating story,' prompted Saddler. 'I 'ear you've got an interesting way of coming into being so to speak!'

'And it appears we've got a fair bit of time on our hands,' Anthony chipped in, ignoring Destiny's look of disapproval.

Boff tapped a long, tapered finger thoughtfully on his pursed, triangular lips.

'Well, of course I don't know how *you* come into being, so that might be interesting too. To us, the way things are just seems normal, although I suppose that doesn't always mean the same thing as good.'

'Does coming into being h-hurt at all?' Destiny stammered nervously.

'Not that I recall, I think it's just like waking up.'

'But you didn't come into being here though?' said Anthony.

'Oh no. Our world is...was called Doodland. It used to be a lovely place – a happy place.' Boff sighed.

'So what happened?'

'Somebody created a cruel leader. Crevitos his name is!' Boff shuddered at the thought. 'It seems he was destined to rule us all. He even changed the name of our world. Doomland it's called now and a very fitting name too, I should say.'

'You know about being "created" then?' asked Anthony surprised.

'Oh yes, in fact I have a good friend – up there.' Boff pointed a willowy finger above his head. 'A very clever man, who was so taken with me when we first met that he did some research. He even drew a few of us himself!'

'Not called the Prof by any chance?' asked Saddler, sounding not even remotely surprised.

Boff brightened visibly.

'You know him?'

'Has the Prof ever been to Doodland?' asked Anthony, by way of reply.

Boff looked cautiously from one to the other before obviously deciding they could be trusted.

'Yes,' he said quietly. 'In fact he helped some of us to come here!'

Looking from one expectant face to the other, Boff sighed, a little dramatically but not, Saddler thought, unpleasurably.

'I'd better start at the beginning I s'pose,' said Boff.

* * *

Boff yawned and stretched vigorously. He opened his eyes to blue sky and those scuddy, white little clouds that make you want to pluck them from the heavens and give them a big hug. He was lying on his back on grass that felt cool and soft to the touch.

How he knew it was his back he was lying on, or that it was grass beneath him and sky above him, he wasn't sure. He just did know and it felt good. Good to be…well…alive. Yes, he was *alive!*

Boff grinned to himself and felt the corners of his mouth stretch. That was a good feeling too. He let his mouth relax and then stretched it into a grin again. Stretch. Relax. Stretch. Relax. It felt marvellous.

'Great feeling, eh, son?' chuckled a throaty voice. It was accompanied by a chorus of laughter and the next thing Boff knew, many hands (tentacles? Paws?) were helping him to his feet.

The next few years were a delight. Doodland, as Boff discovered his home was called, was just the best place to be. He was surrounded by friends, creatures all very different to him physically, yet all bound by a common desire to exist peacefully and happily in their own little haven.

Nobody could really pinpoint when the changes began to happen. Some said it was when the gentle, pattering rain that only fell at night-time and nourished all the plant life, began to fall in harsh bursts during the day.

Before they knew it however, creatures were appearing which seemed to have only one aim point in mind – to cause misery and destruction wherever they went. The landscape began to change. Once colourful, fresh, picturesque views darkened. Where there had been trees and grassy glades, there was now only wasteland. And that wasn't the worst of it.

Creatures which called themselves 'Crevitos henchmen' appeared on the scene. The gentle Creations of Doodland quailed before such menace, such evil as these creatures represented.

And so life on Doodland changed immeasurably.

It soon became clear that there were only two types of Creation: the chosen few – those who elected to become Crevitos's bully boys – and the rest.

As far as Crevitos was concerned, the rest now only had one purpose in life and that was to slave for him, mostly in the mines, which was where Boff had spent many an exhausting and miserable month: toiling, breaking rocks, staggering under heavy loads, and forever transporting endless rubble from one place to another. Mindlessly, back-breakingly, forever fearful of the stinging slash of a whip, signalling that you were not working hard enough, or fast enough, or it happened to be your bad luck that day to pull the wrong face at the wrong moment.

There was no relief. No end in sight; just incessant, interminable, unremitting toil, stretching into the forever after.

In the long huts where the workers grabbed a measly few hours rest, there were rumours; rumours that there was a place somewhere in the far north of the land to which a few lucky Creations had escaped. Nobody knew where or how, but in the stark darkness of the night hours, a glimmer of hope flickered among the inmates.

Boff's ability to daydream had earned him many a flick of the whip, as he imagined himself setting out on a journey to find this special place where Crevitos had no command. A place in his mind that became more green, fresh and beautiful every time he thought about it.

And so it was, that he knew, he *knew*, as soon as he found the box, that something incredible was about to happen.

At first glance, it was not a particularly dazzling box. In fact it was quite ordinary looking; wooden with some pretty carvings on the top.

Boff didn't dare look too closely however, as any cease in activity on his part would bring a whip bearing guard over quicker than winking. The box would be taken from him and that would be that.

Checking carefully to make sure he was not being observed Boff slipped the box under a fair-sized piece of rock. With the rock concealing the box, he carried them over to a nearby cart. Fortunately the cart was almost full. Quickly, he hid the box underneath a heap of rock and began to push the cart along the track to one of the many dumping chutes.

He gasped as a whiplash stung expertly across his back.

'You there!' snarled a fox like creature with fangs that grew up nearly to its ears. 'You call that full?'

'No, Sir. Sorry, Sir. It won't happen again, Sir!' Boff cringed and whimpered and wrung his hands in supplication knowing that, however distasteful, it was the only way a guard might be prepared to let him off more lashes of the whip.

Fortunately, just at that second, a scuffle broke out behind them. With a snarl of 'Snivelling wimp,' the guard turned and stomped off in the direction of the fracas. Taking advantage of the distraction, Boff hurriedly pushed the cart the last few yards to the dumping chute. Glancing around furtively, he surreptitiously rescued the box from its hiding place beneath the rocks and then gave the cart a final shove through an opening in the rock, where it trundled down the chute to yet more exhausted, despairing Creations down below.

In the dimness of the recess, Boff clutched the box to him and slid silently behind a large overhang of rock where he couldn't be seen.

Now for the box. Almost tenderly he traced the carved patterns with a finger, just for a moment afraid to take the plunge and open the lid. Heart beating wildly, he placed his thumb just above the tiny keyhole. It would be locked. Of course it would. No doubt the key had long since disappeared. Applying a little pressure, he was quite shocked when the lid shifted easily upwards.

He took a deep breath, to still his shaking hands. There were wonders, dreams of happiness inside this box, he knew it, just knew…ohhhhhh!

The excitement drained out of him like water down a huge plughole, leaving him feeling weak and not a little foolish.

Well, at least he'd found the key, a small, ornate, sparkling key. Disappointed, he thought at least he might as well see if the key actually fitted. After all, it could still be his little secret. He could hide it here, behind this overhang. A little piece of him no one knew anything about. And maybe one day, one day he'd find out it really did have magical powers and then he would be free of this awful place!

'Imagine,' he whispered to himself as he placed the little silver key into the keyhole, 'just imagine...'

The light that flooded out of the box was enough to bring a whole host of guards down on his back; that Boff knew. But he didn't have time to consider the implications. The dark stain that had rapidly replaced the light was already shrinking. Instinctively, Boff grabbed up the box and stepped forward into the black blot, shutting his eyes tight as he did so.

* * *

Blue sky, fluffy clouds. Blinking in the sunlight, for a moment Boff convinced himself that he had just woken from a horrendous nightmare and Doodland was the same as it had always been. Except he knew that wasn't true. One glance down at his dirty, grime-smeared clothes and the wooden box clutched firmly in his hands told him that it wasn't true.

Maybe this was the future? Maybe Crevitos had gone and Doodland had reverted to its natural state. Or maybe this was the past. Not such a nice thought. That would mean that Crevitos was yet to come!

Boff was startled out of his thoughts by a whistling sound. Instantly fearful, he ducked behind a nearby bush.

The whistling was soon followed round the corner by a small boy. Boff had seen boys before on Doodland, though not quite like this one. This one seemed more – what was the word – solid.

As the boy neared the bush, to Boff's utter amazement, it began to chatter.

'Hello, Squib, hello, hello.' All the leaves seemed to have tiny little voices that all talked in unison. 'We know something you don't know,' they squeaked and giggled.

Squib bent down with his hands on his knees and peered closely at the bush.

'Well you'd better tell me,' he said good naturedly, 'or you know what happens to bushes that keep secrets!'

'Oh no!' squealed the leaves in mock horror. 'Not the tickling, no, no, not that!'

Squib wrinkled his face into a not-very-fierce frown and extended a menacing hand. It touched the leaves lightly and he wriggled his fingers.

'Yes that!' he growled, not very threateningly.

Boff felt the bush shiver with delight and all the little leaves exploded into tiny, tinkly titters again.

It was then he realized that the boy was looking right at him.

'It's okay,' said Squib, 'you can come out. I won't hurt you.'

And strangely, Boff believed him.

CHAPTER THIRTY-TWO

The time spent with Squib and the Prof had been a relief, a delight and an education all rolled into one. The Prof had been fascinated by Boff and had wanted to know everything he could remember about his world and its people – at least as it had been before Crevitos came on the scene.

Boff in turn learnt that he had somehow been transported to a place called Emajen, which, in many ways, was not so very different from his own world.

The Prof apparently knew all about the wooden box. That is to say, not Boff's wooden box precisely; the Prof himself had one almost identical.

'So how does it work exactly?' was Boff's query.

The answer was quite simple. Once the key was inserted in the keyhole of the box, you recited twice the name of where you wanted to be and there you were. *Why* it worked of course was another question and not one the Prof had an answer for.

As far as he knew, they were very rare. He'd only come across one other person on Emajen who had one, although perhaps it was not necessarily something you would tell too many people about.

But Boff was confused.

'I've never even heard of Emajen,' he pointed out, 'let alone knew that I wanted to come here. So how could I have said the name twice?'

The Prof studied Boff closely for a minute.

'Think back,' he said quietly. 'Think back to what exactly happened with the box. You must have said something?'

Boff shut his eyes and, much against his desire, pictured himself back in the mighty mine under the ground.

'Imagine,' he murmured softly and again. 'Imagine...that's it!' he cried. 'I was just thinking how wonderful it would be if the box had magic powers that could spirit me away. I said 'imagine'. I must have said it twice. It's close enough – you think?'

The Prof beamed. 'Most certainly!' He rubbed his beard thoughtfully. 'It rather suggests we should enunciate clearly when using our friend here!' He patted the box fondly.

'Enun...what?'

'Speak clearly,' Squib explained, proud of what he'd learnt from the Prof.

'Oh!' Boff looked thoughtful. 'It's a bit scary. I could have ended up somewhere really awful!'

'Not more awful than Doomland by the sounds of it!' said the Prof. 'Now, the thing is, what are we going to do about the other poor souls in that dreadful place?'

And so they had talked long and hard about how they could return to Doomland to try and rescue some of the other Creations. They had figured that if they asked the box to take them to north Doomland they would be pretty safe from ending up back in the mines. The biggest problem that the Prof could foresee was that there might well be a limit as to how many beings could get through the gateway in one go.

'Will you ask for Doodland or Doomland?' was what Squib wanted to know.

'Good point,' said the Prof.

'Doodland!' said Boff firmly. 'Doomland is only what Crevitos chooses to call it and I firmly believe that one day it will be Doodland once again!'

* * *

Saddler yawned and stretched.

'Good old Prof. It worked then. Are you *all* 'ere? I must say 'e kept it well under 'is 'at. Never once mentioned a word of it to me.'

'We just thought it was safer, you know if nobody knew we were here. But in answer to your question, no we couldn't possibly rescue everyone. To begin with, it was quite easy. We could get about six Creations through the dark splodge at a time and of course, in the north there was no one to notice them go. We were afraid to open a gateway anywhere else in case we got caught, so we thought it would be safest to travel stealthily to the mines at night-times and sneak out a few Creations at a time.'

'That must have been painfully slow,' said Anthony.

'Slow, but relatively secure,' explained Boff. 'The trouble was, as time went on a lot of good, decent Creations turned into spies for Crevitos to try and save themselves from destruction in the mines. Sometimes it was hard to tell who was on our side and who was on his.'

'So what happened?' asked Destiny.

Little sparks flashed briefly inside Boff's head and his light bulbs glowed a pale, sickly, green colour just for a moment.

'The last time we went…we were very nearly caught. We took a chance and opened up nearer to the mines. We tried to save a bit of time. You know maybe get a few more Creations out. But it was our undoing. We'd rounded up enough to go through in two lots. One of Crevitos's sneaks must have seen the gateway open the first time. By the time the second group were ready to go through…' Boff faltered and shuddered, the sickly, green hue returning to his light bulbs.

'I…will…never forget that…face!' He buried his own face in his hands; a picture of such abject misery, that Destiny rushed to his side and put a consoling arm around his shoulders.

'I know. I know about the face!' she murmured soothingly.

Once Boff had calmed a little, Saddler felt it safe to ask, 'Did they follow you? Through the gateway?'

'Not then. Not then,' Boff repeated softly, almost to himself. 'But they saw enough to know it could be done. Worse still, much, much worse, the box was somehow lost in the panic and I very much fear it wouldn't take Crevitos long to figure out how it works.'

'Surely, if he'd found out its secret he'd be here by now trying to take over Emajen like he did Doodland,' suggested Destiny.

'From what you've told me, he's already been here for at least long enough to cause some trouble. But the Prof thinks he's not strong enough to risk a full scale invasion yet. You see Creations aren't terribly strong...' Boff's brain flushed a little pink. 'And we were, still are, mostly gentle folk. We weren't exactly difficult to overcome. Here it's different and Crevitos will need an army, an army that can cross the divide between worlds in much larger numbers.'

'A longer darkness and a bigger 'ole,' said Saddler forebodingly. 'And you can bet that's exactly what 'es working on right now!'

'Oh dear!' Boff's eyes were sad. 'What have we done?'

Destiny looked despairingly at Anthony and tightened her arm protectively around Boff's shoulders.

CHAPTER THIRTY-THREE

'Shh,' Anthony was suddenly alert. 'I can hear someone coming.'

The noise he had heard was really no more than a loud swish, and Destiny was greatly impressed that he'd heard it at all. It heralded the approach of another strange being; a sort of two headed octopus with, as far as Destiny could tell, ten tentacles instead of eight. It was very difficult to count as they kept slithering and wriggling about all over the place.

'Hi, Boff.' The creature smiled with the one mouth its two heads appeared to share, revealing one gleaming white tooth in the centre.

'Hi, Screwy, any news?'

'Screwy?' mouthed Anthony at Destiny.

Destiny grinned and turned back to Boff, keen to know what was going on. Screwy's face had taken on a grim expression.

'A lot of discussion going on,' he told them. 'Eldon He-Haw thinks we should listen to you and help you. The others are not so sure. They say we are well hidden here and they don't want to be involved in any trouble again. They say whatever's going on up there...' he glanced up at the ceiling, '...is none of our business!'

'That's crazy,' yelled Saddler. 'Don't they understand 'oo's behind what's going on? They should know by now that there'll be no 'iding from 'im if 'e finds a way to bring an army 'ere!'

Screwy wriggled all ten tentacles agitatedly.

'They don't want to believe it's *him*!' His voice almost disappeared, so hushed was his whisper.

'Can't *you* do something, Boff? That Eldon said they value your judgement and it was you who brought them here to safety!' demanded Saddler.

All Boff's light bulbs glowed red and his brain was suffused with a violent burgundy flush.

'Oh...oh...I'm not very...I mean, I couldn't...oh...' he stuttered.

Screwy wrapped a tentacle around his friend and the eye in each of his heads stared reprovingly at Saddler.

'Boff here has been braver than anyone I ever met,' he said adamantly. 'The Eldons may value his opinion, but they will insist on working out a number of possible options which will then have to be voted on by all the rest of us. The outcome of the vote is final, no matter what anyone says.'

Destiny looked pleadingly at Boff.

'What are we going to do?' she asked.

Without hesitation, the two Creations answered as one.

'We need to get you out of here!' they said.

CHAPTER THIRTY-FOUR

They all waited anxiously while Boff went to check on the meeting again to see how things were progressing. He reported that the debate was still in full swing and set to continue for some time.

The biggest quandary was that the way out involved crossing through the Great Hall again, where the meeting was currently being held. It was Screwy who suggested that he should create a diversion and give them a chance to slip through without being seen.

Knocking on the door to be let out, Boff explained to the guard that he was now wanted at the meeting and that Boff himself would secure the door before he and Screwy followed in very short order. The strong Creation waved his trunk in acknowledgement and hurried off. Checking that the coast was clear, Boff motioned to the others to follow him. He led them back through the maze of torch-lit passages, until they reached the Great Hall. Despite its enormous size, it was packed with creatures of all shapes and sizes, listening intently to the debate that was being bandied back and forth among the group of Eldons on the raised platform.

As they watched, a Creation standing in the middle of the crowd waved what looked like a white hanky in the air. There was silence while he asked his question and then the Eldons each gave their answer according to their interpretation of the situation.

'No wonder your meetings take so long,' whispered Anthony to Boff.

Screwy, who had disappeared for a moment, now reappeared and waggled a white piece of cloth at them with one of his tentacles.

'Wait 'til I've asked my question –' he beamed – 'and then get going quick!'

'Thanks for this Screwy,' said Boff.

'My pleasure! See you soon, I hope!'

Screwy disappeared once more into the crowd and moments later, they saw a bright yellow tentacle waving its white cloth in the air.

'Don't the Eldons think we ought to help defend Emajen against Crevitos since it's pretty much our fault he found out how to get here in the first place?' queried the voice connected to the tentacle.

There was an immediate uproar throughout the hall, although it was impossible to tell whether in agreement or outrage at Screwy's question.

Without waiting to find out, Boff and the others took the opportunity to slide unobtrusively around the side of the great stone wall and out of the opening at the far end. Boff hurried them up the long passage that led back to their cave, where they squeezed breathlessly through the gap in the overlapping rock.

There was no sound of pursuit, but in any case, Boff was certain that the Creations would be too wary to follow them outside. Even so, they weren't taking any chances and they kept up a steady march until they had made their way down the hillside and into the shelter of the trees.

'So what's the plan?' asked Anthony, once they had stopped to take a breather.

'I think some'ow we'll 'ave to find our way back to the Prof. If Kaz got word to 'im that we needed another map, 'ooever 'e asked to bring it to us would've long since gone back and told 'im we were nowhere to be found. I know it's wasting more time, but I just don't see any 'elp for it!'

'Erm...' Boff coughed politely. 'If it's any help at all, I know the way to the Prof's abode from here.'

'Why the 'ell didn't you say so before?' Saddler muttered irritably.

'He could hardly have known that's where you wanted to go,' Destiny pointed out.

'No, no, you're right. I'm sorry, Boff. It's all this time we've lost already and now we've got to squander more going right back to where we started! So 'ow long will it take from 'ere?'

'Oh, about – let's see, half a day perhaps.'

'Half a day?' Destiny looked perplexed. 'How can that be, when it took us so long to get here!'

'I think you'll find we've let ourselves be thoroughly befogged by this 'ere Crevitos character!' groaned Saddler. 'We're really going to 'ave to be on our mettle from now on!'

Boff gave Destiny a puzzled look.

'Translation?' she asked. He nodded.

'Saddler means we've been led astray by Crevitos and we need to be much more careful from now on.'

'S'wot I said innit?' huffed Saddler.

Boff however just nodded gravely.

'I think,' he said, 'that the more Crevitos learns, the stronger and more powerful he becomes. I don't know what happened a while back, but suddenly he seemed to have a lot more power. It doesn't surprise me that he's been causing you grief.'

'Well, the longer we stay around here, the more likely it is that he'll catch up with us again,' said Anthony. He stood up and dusted himself off. 'Why do you think Crevitos has any interest in Emajen at all, Boff?'

Boff considered carefully. 'I think he's such a Mad-Creation that he just wants to conquer world after world until or unless he's stopped. Why Emajen? I'm not sure. Perhaps just because *we* came here or maybe it has some other importance. Either way, I don't think it will be long before he gets what he wants!' Boff's brain fizzed with the emotion of it all.

There was a silence as the others considered the import of what he'd just said.

'Best get going then!' said Saddler.

They shouldered their belongings and set off once more for the Prof's house.

CHAPTER THIRTY-FIVE

'Ah, I was rather afraid something like this might happen,' said the Prof, seeming not at all surprised when they turned up on his doorstep. 'Obviously we mustn't underestimate the increase in power our evil friend has gained!'

Tea was made, biscuits produced, and provisions re-stocked. Squib had paid a visit to Nebiré with another copy of the map. She had very kindly worked a charm to protect this one from being tampered with.

'Handy,' said Anthony, who was still a bit bemused by some of the more mystical aspects of Emajen.

'Before you go,' said the Prof, 'I have a couple of other little items for you that I've just finished working on. They may be of some use. They need a little explanation, so before that there's also something else, which I think will please you greatly, Destiny. This way.'

With a quizzical look at the others, Destiny followed the Prof. He led her through his kitchen to the back door. The others traipsed after them.

'I bet I can guess,' grinned Anthony.

The Prof had a small, neat, pretty cottage type garden, beyond which stretched fields and hills as far as the eye could see. He led Destiny through a smart wooden gate at the back of his garden and there, munching grass to his heart's content was...

'Kaz!' shrieked Destiny, hurrying forward to throw her arms around him.

Horses don't have the muscle structure to smile, on Earth or on Emajen, but he certainly radiated pleasure even though he said gruffly, 'I knew you wouldn't get far without me!'

Once Destiny had been persuaded to tear herself away from Kaz, the Prof took them into his living room and sat them down comfortably, while he rooted around for two objects that he thought might assist them in their travels.

To Anthony, he gave a round globe that looked rather like an opaque crystal ball.

'It doesn't tell the future I'm afraid.' The Prof smiled. 'But it will shed light and warmth – all you have to do is ask.'

Destiny was given a ring in the shape of a coiled snake, with diamond eyes that glittered and sparkled. It was beautiful.

'It's not just a pretty trinket, although I confess, I do rather like the sparkly eyed touch. More importantly, it has the power to heal whoever wears it. You just have to rub your thumb around the coil from head to tail and it will release enough of the natural endorphins in your body to cure most ills. However...' here he held up a warning finger, '...its power is limited, so use it sparingly!'

By this time it was very late, so after a very welcome bath and a hot meal, the travellers collapsed into their beds and slept dreamlessly until dawn.

CHAPTER THIRTY-SIX

This time, they took only what they could carry in their rucksacks. They had lost the cart and it was obvious that there were going to be parts of the journey where it would be difficult for Kaz to follow.

The nator walked along with them for a short way to be companionable he said, although of course it had nothing what-so-ever to do with the fact that Destiny was plying him with carrot treats the whole time.

At last, with a flick of his tail and a warm affectionate snuffle in Destiny's ear, Kaz set off at a sedate canter back to the Prof's and the comfort of his grassy field.

The travellers made good progress now that they actually had a map that led them in the right direction. As dusk began to fall, they reached a landmark they had been aiming for and were chuffed to have made it so far without any mishap.

It was beginning to get quite chilly, so they headed for a clump of trees to give them some shelter. Without any spoken agreement, no one suggested finding any accommodation. Nebiré might have been able to protect the map, but it was unlikely that she would have any control over what might happen on the rest of their journey.

The vision of what they had encountered last time at the inn was still fresh in their minds and was not an experience they would willingly repeat.

They set up camp, but decided they would have to forego the pleasure of a hot drink. Lighting a fire might be dodgy. Crevitos's creatures could be anywhere and they didn't want to announce their presence if they could avoid it.

Anthony dug in his rucksack and carefully pulled out the globe the Prof had given him.

'I wonder how bright this is?' he mused. 'I should probably

have checked it out before.'

'Try just asking it for warmth,' suggested Destiny. 'Maybe you can get light and warmth separately?'

'Could we have some warmth, please' asked Anthony, and nearly dropped the globe as it glowed a pale red in his hands.

Within just a few moments a cheering heat began to radiate from the globe and the group huddled around it, amazed and delighted by the amount of heat such a small object could disperse.

'Good ole Prof!' said Saddler, and they all heartily agreed.

The night passed peacefully. Comforted by the soothing warmth that emanated from the globe, they all slept dreamlessly. Destiny half awoke only once, saw the pale radiance of the orb and, smiling, drifted back to sleep again.

Although quite cold, the day dawned bright and clear; a soft pastel sun promising some measure of warmth as the day wore on. Breakfast was consumed quickly and in companionable silence. Just before they set off again, Anthony took the egg timer out and looked at it thoughtfully. The rainbow coloured sand was now split in equal parts between the top of the timer and the bottom.

'Looks like we'd better get a move on,' said Anthony seriously. The group looked sombre. They had wasted so much time and, even if the rest of the trip went smoothly, they still had to work out what to do about the Natorqua. Shouldering their backpacks, they set off determinedly on the next leg of their journey.

CHAPTER THIRTY-SEVEN

After a brief stop for lunch, the travellers headed for their next landmark, an ancient market town that was rumoured to have been there, so Saddler said, since anyone could remember.

He filled them in as they were going along.

'According to Nebiré, it's a strange old place. Used to be a proper market, full of ordinary folks coming to buy and sell their wares. Now, rumour 'as it, there's more sly dealings going on than enough!'

'But you've never been there?'

'Not me, never 'ad the need, but the Prof told me all about it. Used to be one of Nebiré's old 'unting grounds too, but as you've seen she doesn't get out much these days.'

'So why are we heading for this delightful place?' enquired Boff, as they reached the outskirts of the town.

'I've got a friend of Nebiré's to see; about a mile off over there. Least I can do after all 'er 'elp. Then we can stock up on provisions in the town.'

Strange was hardly a sufficient word for the place they found themselves in. From a distance it looked like any old town with market stalls ranged around the cobbled main square. But as they approached, they could see that the individuals frequenting the market place could hardly be described as 'ordinary folk'.

They could feel the charged atmosphere, almost as though at any moment a violent thunderstorm might rent the air. They all shivered.

'Magic,' murmured Saddler, 'an' not necessarily the good kind neither. Right, listen up. I'll be as quick as I can. 'Ave a wander round, but don't talk to anyone and whatever you do, don't eat or drink anything!' So saying, he hurried off.

The children and Boff began to wend their way amongst the various stalls. They were afraid they would look very out of place in their ordinary clothes, aware they might attract unwanted attention. But they needn't have worried. Most of the market's inhabitants were too intent on their own business to pay any attention to them.

They gazed around them fascinated. No shape, size or colour of individual seemed unrepresented. Some of the outfits looked like witches' clothes straight out of a film, whilst amongst the varying shades of black and grey there were flashes of vibrant colour and people in flamboyant attire that might easily have been designed for a carnival.

'Look at that!' hissed Destiny as one particularly striking individual, about seven foot tall, swirled past them in a blaze of red, purple and gold. The individual in question turned and flashed her the most amazing, brilliant white smile, before melting away into the crowd. Destiny blushed so furiously she thought she might self-combust. Anthony grabbed her arm and dragged her behind a nearby stall.

'Twit!' he said affectionately.

'He must have had supersonic hearing!' complained Destiny.

Anthony and Boff exchanged smiles.

'What?' Destiny frowned.

'Come on,' said Anthony, 'let's find somewhere a bit quieter, before someone gets us into a whole lot of trouble!'

Leaving the stalls behind them, they walked down a narrow, cobbled alleyway marvelling at all the ancient, drunken looking houses. Destiny enthused, her embarrassment forgotten. Roofs sagged and walls bowed, but somehow, despite all that, the wooden beams and whitewashed walls looked as though they would quite happily weather a few more hundred years yet.

But…everywhere seemed quiet and totally deserted.

'Maybe everyone goes to the market?' suggested Boff hopefully.

'Or maybe everyone shuts up shop and stays indoors until the market's over!' Anthony shuddered. 'I don't like the feel of this place. Anyway, it's beginning to get dark and Saddler said he wouldn't be long. He's probably wondering where on earth we've got to.'

They wound their way back through the cramped cobbled streets, until they could hear the hue and cry of the market once more. Judging by the volume, it was still very much in full swing despite the creeping dusk.

They were just in view of the first stalls, when Destiny saw something in a dull recess that caught her attention.

'Look!' she said, pointing.

The smallest monkey they had ever seen, dressed in a tiny soldier's uniform was performing juggling tricks with bananas and oranges. They watched enthralled for a couple of moments, until the monkey accidentally dropped one of the bananas. Instantly it scampered to the farthest length of a chain that they could now see was attached to one of its legs. It cowered, tiny hands covering its face. A wizened old man stepped out of the shadows with a raised stick in his hand.

'Useless beast!' he growled, and was just about to bring the stick crashing down on the unfortunate creature, when he noticed the group watching him. Without a word he turned and hurried back the way he had come.

Before the others could stop her, Destiny had rushed forward.

'You poor thing!' she cried.

The monkey raised its head from its hands and peered at her uncertainly. Fortunately, the chain was attached to a small leather band around the monkey's leg and so Destiny talked soothingly to the little fellow while she undid the tiny buckles that secured it there. Free at last, the tiny monkey leapt gratefully into her arms and snuggled there, chattering softly.

'Fleas,' pointed out Anthony, grinning.

'Shush.' Destiny scowled.

'When you two have finished canoodling, I think this might be a good time to get out of here. That old man didn't look too happy when he left and I'm pretty certain he's not going to be any more cheerful when he comes back and finds you've let his monkey go!'

'Well, what do you expect...?' Destiny began to argue, but she was cut short as the monkey leapt to the floor and scurried off. It ran a few yards and then stopped, looking back at them pointedly.

'Looks like he wants us to follow,' said Boff, somewhat unnecessarily.

Anthony raised his eyebrows. 'Here we go again,' he muttered as the three of them hurriedly followed in the monkey's wake.

CHAPTER THIRTY-EIGHT

Just on the edge of the town there was a tavern. With frequent stops to check that the children were still following him, it was here that the little monkey led them. It sped through the swing doors, across the dusty floor and leapt straight up onto the bar.

Anthony, Destiny and Boff hovered uncertainly in the doorway. The place was gloomy and uninviting and seemed to be full of dark little niches, where most of the inhabitants looked as though they were furtively discussing dodgy deals. But the bar tender seemed jolly enough. As soon as he appeared, his big, round face broke into a beaming smile at the sight of the little monkey. For his part, the little fellow leapt at once into the barman's arms and chattered furiously, pointing at the group in the doorway and patting winningly at the barman's fluffy white beard.

After a minute or two, the barman's grin became even broader and he gestured expansively at the children and Boff to come in. He led them to a table in a cosy little nook and loomed cheerily over them, rubbing his meaty hands.

'Well, now,' he said effusively, 'my little friend over there –' he gestured towards the monkey who was contentedly nibbling at nuts on the bar – 'tells me that you've been most kind…most kind! That dratted man keeps catching him and forcing him to do those ridiculous juggling tricks. I'll get hold of him one day – and when I do…' The barman's face darkened for a moment, but then brightened again almost immediately.

'Enough of that! The least I can do is to offer you some refreshment.' He looked first at Boff and then at the children. 'I think I have the very thing for you youngsters. Warm you up a treat.'

He bustled off before they could say a word, moving surprising quickly for a man of his girth.

'This is supremely weird!' said Destiny.

'Is there anything that hasn't been weird since we met Saddler?' queried Anthony.

'I don't want to be a misery guts,' Boff said tentatively, 'but Saddler was most insistent that we shouldn't eat or drink anything!'

'You're right,' said Anthony, 'but that was from the market stalls. Surely a tavern should be safe enough?'

'But still...'

'Shhh,' hissed Destiny, 'he's coming back!'

The barman was carrying a tray with tall glass mugs, full of something that looked a bit like ice-cream sundaes. There were also huge cakes of some description that might have been chocolate muffins. With his beaming smile, the barman placed the glasses and plates in front of each of them and then stood back with a look of tremendous satisfaction on his face. Suddenly, he threw his hands up in the air.

'Oh, napkins, forgot the napkins. Back in a jiffy.'

Destiny looked worriedly at Anthony.

'I'm not sure about this!'

'It's going to look extremely rude if we go without touching anything though,'

'If we drink up quickly,' said Boff, eyeing up the cakes hungrily, 'we can say we're in a bit of a hurry. No harm done.'

The others agreed as the barman returned with the napkins.

'Anything else I can get you?' he enthused.

They all thanked him several times and assured him there wasn't. He hovered by them, obviously keen for them to tuck in.

Boff was the first to give way. He supped some of the liquid from the tall glass. His eyes closed for a moment, as though he were thinking deeply. Then he opened them again and beamed at the others.

'Delicious!' he announced.

The barman laughed delightedly and hurried away to serve

another customer.

Boff seemed fine, in fact he was tucking into his cake as though he hadn't had a meal in weeks.

Anthony shrugged and sipped his drink. It turned out to be a sort of hot chocolate, but with a much nuttier flavour. It had the consistency of a thick milkshake and was topped with something that looked like whipped cream, but was somehow warm. Once they started drinking, the children found it was so delicious that they couldn't stop.

* * *

As Anthony stood in the corral and watched Toby, his brow wrinkled into a frown. Destiny and Boff both perched on the fence, watching silently. Anthony looked back at them and then once more at Toby. Something just wasn't right.

For the moment Toby was nibbling contentedly at the small, pale yellow, buttermilk flowers that blanketed the coral grass like creamy custard over an apple tart. Anthony took a step towards him, without being entirely sure why he did so.

Immediately, the mild, peaceful scene altered. Toby's head whipped up instantly alert. His bright amber eyes bored into Anthony's and his lips creased menacingly upwards at the corners, revealing vicious, gleaming fangs. Toby's tail began to lash wildly from side to side. He pawed with a front hoof, all the while staring intently at Anthony. Mesmerising his prey.

Just like a cat might.

But Toby wasn't a cat, was he?

Anthony looked desperately back at Destiny and Boff. They were pointing furiously towards Toby; mouths contorted in silent screams that nonetheless slashed the air with their meaning.

Painfully slowly Anthony turned once more. Toby was still now, apart from a slight pleasurable quiver of his whiskers. On his back sat a tall, imposing figure with a stunning face and a wide, cruel smile.

For reasons Anthony couldn't fathom, he seemed startlingly familiar.

There was an odd rumbling sound that Anthony couldn't place. And then he realized...it was a purr. Toby was emitting a deep, contented, rumbling purr. And the figure on his back grinned and his grin grew wider and wider...

CHAPTER THIRTY-NINE

Anthony was cold. He was stiff and he could hear a disturbing groaning sound. His head ached and his mouth was unpleasantly dry and sour. He shifted his weight in an attempt to sit up from his cramped position on the hard floor. The groaning noise increased in intensity and he suddenly realized that it was coming from him.

Defeated for a moment, he lay back and drifted into a light doze before waking once again. This time he stayed still until his eyes began to accustom themselves to the gloom. Cautiously raising himself up on one elbow, he tried to make sense of his surroundings. He appeared to be in some kind of room, full of objects that he couldn't make out as yet. Not too far away were two bundles that looked like heaps of rags in the murky dimness. One moved slightly and there was another groaning sound, this time not coming from him.

'Destiny?' His voice croaked with dryness. Head throbbing, Anthony stiffly eased himself to his feet. He approached the two bundles cautiously and realized that they were indeed Destiny and Boff.

They were obviously still fast asleep and so Anthony decided that he would explore the surroundings. He knew there was light filtering through from somewhere otherwise they would have been in complete darkness. He felt his way carefully along rows of what appeared to be shelves. Turning a corner, the light increased a little, which was when Anthony espied a small, grimy window, set high in the wall at the far end of the room.

It was also when everything clicked into place.

The shelves were actually wine racks. The other indiscernible objects turned out to be crates and barrels and there were all kinds of other odds and ends.

Of course! They were in the cellar of the pub; the pub that the monkey had led them to! Was this another of Crevitos's tricks to waylay them? And the corral – was that a bizarre hallucination or just a dream?

Right now, Anthony had two more pressing problems. He needed to figure a way out and he needed a drink. He searched through the crates and found some bottles that looked as though they might contain water. Gratefully he untwisted the cap and sniffed at the contents. Reassured he gulped down the refreshing liquid, feeling it soothe his parched mouth and throat. Grabbing a couple more, he made his way carefully back to where Boff and Destiny still lay.

Boff was beginning to stir, his light bulbs flickering on and off as he struggled to come to consciousness.

Gently, Anthony held a bottle of water to Boff's lips and encouraged him to drink. After a few moments, Boff's eyes opened fully. Before he could say anything, Anthony put a warning finger to his lips.

'We're in the cellar of the tavern. Do you remember what happened?' he whispered softly.

Boff nodded.

'I'm not sure anyone would hear us down here, the walls seem pretty thick – but just in case we'd better keep our voices down. All the while they think we're still out for the count, I guess we'll be left alone.'

'Who's they?' whispered Boff.

'I'm not sure. The barman? The old man with the monkey? Maybe even Crevitos! What I am sure of is that somehow we've got to get out of here and find Saddler.'

Boff nodded his head. His brain wobbled and he grimaced and reached for the bottle of water again.

'There's a small window,' Anthony continued, 'just at the back there. It's too small for me, but if we can get it open, you might be able to squeeze through.'

Boff scrambled to his feet. 'What are we waiting for?' he said.

Anthony left a bottle of water beside Destiny hoping that, if she woke before he got back, she would realize he had put it there and not panic at finding herself on her own.

Quickly, he and Boff worked their way to the back of the cellar. Anthony surveyed the window. It was quite high up, but there were plenty of crates they could use to climb on. What concerned him, even if they could get the window open, was what the drop would be like on the other side. There was only one way to find out. As stealthily as they could, he and Boff began to stack some of the crates so that they formed a kind of stairway up to the window.

Anthony climbed up first, testing the way carefully to make sure that the crates were secure. Reaching the window, he peered out through the grime. From what little he could see, the window gave out onto a small courtyard that thankfully looked as though it was deserted. The cellar was obviously below ground level and so in fact there would be hardly any drop at all from the window to the ground outside – so far, so good. Now all they had to do was get the window open.

Tentatively, he gave it a push to see if there was any give in it at all or whether it was solidly wedged. To his utter astonishment the window shifted slightly. He pushed again, a little harder this time. With just the smallest of creaks, the window opened a crack.

Anthony looked back down at Boff. This was too easy. Something didn't seem quite right. Anthony waited, breath held, but there was nothing. The courtyard remained deserted. He climbed down off the crates again and looked at an enquiring Boff.

'I don't like this! Looking at the dirt on that window, you'd think it would be jammed solid.'

'Maybe it's used regularly, just not cleaned?' Boff suggested helpfully.

'But why would you leave it unlocked? It's an obvious escape route!'

'Maybe they didn't expect us to wake up so soon...or maybe they thought it was too small for any of us to get through...or maybe they just forgot? It can't have been easy shifting three sleeping bodies down here, especially with all those other folk in the tavern!'

'Unless they're all in it together!' said Anthony grimly.

'Whatever the reason, we have to get out of here and the window appears to be our only option.'

'You're right. We'll just have to risk it!'

Climbing nimbly up the crates again, Anthony peered out into the courtyard once more. Nothing. He gave the window a hard shove, wobbling dangerously on the crates as he did so. The hinges creaked once and then light was flooding through the small aperture into the cellar below.

He clambered back down.

'It's up to you now. Just be careful okay!'

Boff grinned. 'If I get caught the chances are they'll only put me back in here again!'

He shinned up the crates and in a flash of tartan shorts had disappeared through the window. Anthony climbed up after him and pulled the window to, leaving it just open enough in case Boff needed to get back in that way. He felt the gloom settle back on the cellar now that the light had all but been extinguished. Then he made his way back to Destiny to see how she was doing. He had no idea whether Boff would be able to find Saddler, but he figured that he and Destiny were probably in for a long wait.

Destiny was just beginning to stir. Anthony felt a pang of guilt as he knelt down beside her. She hadn't been happy about any of this and it was he who had persuaded her to go along with it. It was his fault they were here; his fault they were in this mess. And he knew why. The Natorqua fascinated him, just as the horses back home did. And if they could fathom out what was going wrong with the Natorqua's minds, what a challenge!

But he had been wrong to involve Destiny...

His thoughts were interrupted by a loud groan from beside him. Destiny opened her eyes and winced.

'Erg,' she muttered huskily.

Anthony helped her to sit up and offered her the bottle of water. She drank greedily.

'What's going on?' she said at last. 'Is this real, or was the corral real? What was that animal? I thought it was Toby to start with, but then – then there was...' She shuddered.

'I think we had the same dream,' Anthony said quietly. 'And I think it might have been some kind of message or warning!'

'We need to find Saddler! Where are we?' Destiny asked, taking stock of her surroundings at last.

Anthony explained. He was just saying he hoped that Boff could find Saddler, when there was an ominous creaking sound from the top of the cellar steps.

Slowly, the cellar door began to open.

CHAPTER FORTY

There was no time to hide. Anthony looked around frantically for something they could defend themselves with. Destiny however pulled him down roughly.

'Pretend you're still sleeping,' she hissed, 'it's our only chance!'

Feigning deep slumber, they waited breathlessly. Would whoever it was notice that there were now only two of them? Would they be fooled by the motionless bodies?

They waited.

'Cor, sleeping on the job, whatever next!'

'Saddler!'

Destiny and Anthony both sprang to their feet, overjoyed to see Saddler again.

'But how...?'

'Oof...' Destiny's legs crumpled beneath her and her look of joy turned to one of complete surprise.

'Destiny?'

At once, Saddler and Anthony were at her side. They helped her to her feet and sat her down on one of the crates. She thanked them and smiled wanly.

'Just came over a bit weak for a moment. I'm fine!'

'Hmm,' said Saddler, 'just left young Boff sitting outside for the same reason. Best we get out of 'ere I reckon, then you can fill me in.'

'What about the barman?'

'You'll see,' said Saddler grimly.

Destiny and Anthony followed Saddler warily up the cellar steps. It was odd that he didn't seem to be showing any caution at all. At the top of the steps the door gave way to into a smaller room, obviously some kind of storage area.

With no hesitation at all, Saddler marched through the storeroom and pushed the far door open. Anthony tensed, unsure what to expect as their eyes adjusted to the muted daylight in the pub.

He and Destiny looked around nonplussed. The tavern was deserted. Chairs stacked on tables looked as though they had been there for some time judging by the vast cobwebs strung between them. There was dust everywhere. The whole place looked neglected and forlorn.

Destiny leaned hard against the bar. She swayed a little and Saddler steadied her. Anthony rubbed his eyes, a nagging throb beginning to form at his temples once again. Without a word, Saddler helped Destiny across the floor to the swing doors, which creaked loudly as he pushed them open.

They blinked in the bright sunlight and then gazed in disbelief at what they saw. The tavern itself was one of only a handful of derelict looking buildings. There were no stalls and the cobbled streets were unrecognisable under the littered remains of charred and wrecked dwellings.

'Bamboozled again!' said Saddler angrily, and without another word he strode off in the direction of the trees leaving Destiny, Boff and Anthony to struggle after him.

By the time they had caught up with him, Saddler had lit a small fire and, although he still looked grim, was whistling softly under his breath while he made some tea.

At first, they all sat in silence, each mulling over the events of the last few hours.

Then Saddler said wearily, 'Seems like Crevitos 'as managed to delay us yet again! I found Nebiré's chap exactly where she said 'e would be and guess what? 'E told me the town 'ad been burnt to the ground more than a year ago. Been rebuilt, 'asn't it, but about three miles in that direction!' He pointed with a finger that shook with worry and frustration.

'So how...' began Boff

'Don't ask me. Seems like this 'ere Crevitos is getting stronger by the day if 'e can make a 'ole town appear where it isn't! Now, you'd better tell me what 'appened to you!'

Anthony told Saddler their story, missing out nothing. He took full responsibility for encouraging the others to eat and drink at the tavern.

Saddler just grunted. 'Seems like Crevitos would 'ave found some way of making it 'appen anyway.'

By now the sun was at its zenith and they were glad of the tendrils of warmth that filtered through the mottled leaves.

Saddler had been given clear instructions by Nebiré's friend to get to the existing town and he proposed that he would go and stock up on provisions for the rest of the journey. The others weren't too sure about being left again, but Saddler was adamant.

'An hour there and an hour back. Three hours all told and I'll be back well before it gets dark.'

'I really think we should stay together,' said Destiny, jumping to her feet. The sudden movement made her head spin and she sat down again in a hurry.

'Think I'll be quicker on my own,' said Saddler. 'You lot need to get your strength back and drink plenty of water. Whatever you were given ain't out of your systems yet!'

'We could use Destiny's ring,' suggested Boff excitedly.

'But we're not really ill,' said Anthony. 'Just a bit...'

'Woozy,' supplied Saddler wryly. 'Anthony's right, anyway I think it's best if you lot steer clear of towns for a bit. I'll be as quick as I can. Just don't *go* anywhere, eat or drink *anything* that isn't yours or talk to *any* strangers!'

'No, Sir!' chorused the others, which earned them a very withering look from Saddler.

He shouldered his bag and turned to go.

'Saddler,' Destiny called after him. He turned and she slipped the ring the Prof had given her off her finger.

'Take this with you. I'm not sure why, but just in case...'

With a short nod of thanks, Saddler turned and disappeared into the trees.

CHAPTER FORTY-ONE

For a while, Saddler strode purposely through the forest, intent only on reaching his destination, his mind full of all the events that had occurred since he had met Destiny and Anthony. They were a tough pair of cookies and already he looked upon them as friends. He could barely even admit to himself how worried he'd been when he'd returned to find a shell of a town and no sign of them or Boff.

The dappled sunlight teased the leaves and the undergrowth. Everything was still and calm. And quiet. Too quiet. It suddenly dawned on him that there were no sounds in the forest at all. Even Nebiré's woods had seemed less eerie than here.

Without warning, he stopped dead in his tracks and swung around to glance behind him. He thought he caught the flicker of a movement out of the corner of one eye, but it could have just been his overwrought imagination. Shrugging his shoulders, as if to dismiss his thoughts, Saddler began to walk again being careful to maintain the same pace he had before. But he was wary and his eyes flickered constantly from side to side, ready to pick up the slightest disturbance in the trees.

After a short while, he stumbled deliberately, casting a furtive glance behind him. And there, a definite shadow, slipping noiselessly behind the shelter of a nearby tree. Grim faced, Saddler marched forwards once again, heading for an area just ahead where the foliage was denser. As soon as he was sure he must be out of sight, he ducked down behind a thick shrub and waited.

He didn't have to wait long before a surprisingly portly figure crept into view. From the description Anthony had given him, Saddler was in no doubt at all that this must be the infamous barman.

The barman stopped and looked around, listening intently.

He stood no more than a few steps away from where Saddler crouched, but as he turned to look in the opposite direction, Saddler took a chance. He picked up a hefty stone and lobbed it as hard as he could up ahead. By pure chance, it landed on a small twig, which cracked with much the same effect as if it had been trodden on. The barman's head whipped round and, with no hesitation, he slipped forwards into the trees. Saddler was after him like a shot and now the hunter had become the hunted – or so Saddler believed.

The barman continued to forge his way ahead, slipping nimbly from tree to tree as though he knew exactly where his quarry was. Under different circumstances, it might have struck Saddler as odd that the barman kept moving steadily on with no certainty, now that he obviously couldn't see Saddler, that he was actually going in the right direction. But Saddler didn't have time to muse on the whys and wherefores. He was focussed entirely on seeing where the barman was going.

After some while, the trees thinned a little and Saddler had to hang back to avoid the risk of being seen. Suddenly, without warning, he stepped out into a patch of wild, purple ferns that waved serenely around his waist, although Saddler could feel no breeze. The area he stood in was circular, no more than a hundred feet across and right in the middle stood the most enormous tree he had ever seen. Its girth alone took up nearly half the clearing and it towered up so high that its tallest branches disappeared from view amongst the clouds.

Saddler stood transfixed, taken off his guard, when the stout, grinning figure of the barman stepped out from behind the enormous tree trunk.

'Welcome.' He beamed at Saddler. 'You haven't met my friend, have you?'

But before Saddler had a chance to see who the 'friend' might be he was shoved roughly from behind. At the same moment, a yawning hole appeared in the trunk of the tree, accompanied by a bright light and swiftly followed by a familiar, pulsating splodge of black.

Saddler stumbled forward, unable to stop his own momentum and was pitched helplessly through the darkness.

CHAPTER FORTY-TWO

Pictures swam in and out of Saddler's vision that made no sense at all. They made him feel nauseous, so he closed his eyes tightly and the darkness helped. He drifted in and out of a doze and was finally woken by an odd scraping noise. He risked opening his eyes just a sliver, fearful of the shifting images that had made him feel so queasy before.

This time however, all was still and he realized that he was lying on a small bed. The room he was in had curved walls and was lit by the soft amber glow of a solitary lantern.

The scraping sound happened again, causing Saddler to lift his head sharply. A pain shot through his head and he winced, putting his hand up to feel a sizeable lump on the back of his skull.

'My apologies,' soothed a disembodied voice, 'that was most unnecessary and decidedly clumsy!'

The voice rippled silkily, but Saddler could hear the menace beneath the surface. Moving his head more carefully this time, he focussed at last on the owner of the voice, who sat at a desk, the contours of which were purposely curved to follow the shape of the wall. The speaker stood, moving the chair as he did so, the carved wooden legs producing a harsh scraping noise on the flagstones.

The figure was tall and imposing. Where had he heard that before, wondered Saddler?

The figure moved closer, its lithe body rippling with grace and power. It towered over Saddler and the beautiful, strong face leered down at him, eyebrow arched, mocking smile giving the lie to his expressions of concern.

'Crevitos!' breathed Saddler. He tried to sit up, but collapsed again with a groan.

'The very same,' smirked Crevitos. He leant over to retrieve something from a small table set by the bed. With surprising gentleness, he lifted Saddler's head and commanded, 'Drink!'

Looking up into Crevitos's face, Saddler realized there was very little point in refusing. He certainly didn't have the strength to fight Crevitos off and if he was supposed to be dead, he no doubt would be by now.

As though tracking Saddler's thoughts, Crevitos twisted his mouth into a wry smile and held the small phial to Saddler's lips.

'Herbal,' was Crevitos's only comment.

Which could, Saddler thought ruefully, mean anything; after all, arsenic was herbal.

A brief bitterness touched his taste buds, followed by a warmth that tracked its way all the way down his oesophagus and into his stomach. Crevitos then busied himself with something at his desk, whilst Saddler rested his head back on the pillow and closed his eyes. In no time at all however, Saddler's headache eased and the warmth created by the drink transformed into a glowing feeling of well-being.

Saddler opened his eyes and studied the powerful back of Crevitos, as he sat straight, but relaxed, on his desk chair.

'Feeling better?' Crevitos turned to look at Saddler. Every movement he made was agile and unhurried. He exuded power and a supreme confidence in himself. He has the knack of making you feel very insignificant, Saddler thought.

'Are you ready?'

Saddler detected a certain excitement in Crevitos's voice. He sat up, grateful that the pounding in his head had ceased. He looked at Crevitos warily.

'Come!' That half-smile flickered again. 'There's something I want to show you.'

Even with his newfound energy, the steps down from Crevitos's eyrie seemed interminable and Saddler's legs were trembling by the time they reached the bottom. Crevitos appeared to be totally unaffected and when he looked at Saddler that mocking smile never seemed to be far from his lips. They crossed a rough stone floor to a heavy iron gate.

'We have a way still to go,' said Crevitos, thoroughly enjoying the look of dismay on Saddler's face, 'but you'll no doubt be glad to hear that it doesn't involve any more steps.'

Crevitos opened the gate to a very small, box-like room and unhesitatingly stepped inside. Saddler followed him suspiciously, unable to fathom how this tiny, square and completely empty room could lead anywhere.

At first glance he could see no means of exit other than an iron gate through which they had just passed and which Crevitos now clanged noisily shut behind them.

Crevitos pulled a lever by the side of the gate.

Before Saddler could utter a sound, the bottom dropped out of his world!

Thrown off balance, Saddler stumbled but was steadied by Crevitos's vice-like grip.

'An amazing invention!'

Saddler could hear the amusement in Crevitos's voice and was annoyed at his own feeling of helplessness.

'It's called a lift,' Crevitos continued, 'an ingenious way of going either up or down – don't you think?'

Still struggling to will his stomach down to its natural position, Saddler was in no mood to be impressed. In all his travels, strangely he had never actually been in such a contraption. He wasn't sure he'd missed much.

The lift's descent seemed as interminable as their previous trek down the stairs but, once Saddler's stomach had settled, he had to grudgingly admit it was a lot easier on the legs.

Finally, the contraption came to a grinding, jolting halt and the murk of the lift was replaced by a flickering glow. Crevitos slid open the heavy iron gate and surged forwards with his customary energy.

Saddler, who had very little option but to follow, stepped more cautiously out of the lift, trying to gauge his surroundings. They were clearly very deep underground; vast tunnels hewn out of the rock stretched in every direction, lit by blazing torches. Saddler knew about the mines of course from Boff. Was he going to be put to work down here? He could think of no other reason for being here and yet, somehow it made no sense.

Crevitos disappeared round a bend and Saddler, anxious not to be stranded alone in this vast underground labyrinth, hurried to catch him up. As he rounded the corner, Saddler was amazed to see a huge network of rail tracks, which obviously carried the workers to the mines and back. At one end of the cavern, a gigantic stone stairway ascended round in a spiral until it disappeared out of sight.

Following his gaze, Crevitos smirked.

'Be grateful we came down in the lift. My slaves don't have that luxury!'

Saddler wondered whether it was day or night, but there was no way of telling down here and Saddler had no idea how long he'd been unconscious for. Not to mention, time could be completely different here to Emajen. Again, Crevitos almost seemed to read his thoughts.

'There is no day or night here, for those who toil in my mines,' he said scornfully, 'only work and sleep. While one slave sleeps, the other works. How else would I extract the vast quantities of diamond I need?'

He gestured to Saddler to sit in one of the empty carts. It began to trundle slowly along one of the tracks, to the point where it divided into two separate tunnels.

Boff had told Saddler about the 'diamond' that was Crevitos's driving passion and he also knew that it was of no value in Doomland. Despite himself, Saddler was curious.

'So, what do you need all this diamond for?' he asked in what he hoped was a casual voice.

'Ah, that's exactly what I want to show you! This track –'
he indicated the one that disappeared off to the left – 'leads to
one of the mines. The one we are about to follow is far more
interesting.' Crevitos smiled and the effect was one of startling
beauty, a stark contrast to the cold malicious gleam in his eyes.
He folded his arms and would say no more until they had
reached their destination.

CHAPTER FORTY-THREE

The cart ran steadily, as the track twisted and turned, sometimes going downwards and sometimes slightly up. On the whole, though, Saddler was certain they were descending further still.

To begin with, the thick silence was only broken by the rattle of the cart's wheels on the track, until Saddler became aware of the distant hum of voices. As they drew closer, the noise increased and he could also hear the clash of metal and then other indefinable wailing sounds that chilled him to the core.

They rounded a final bend. What greeted Saddler's eyes took his breath away.

Crevitos stopped the cart and watched Saddler's face with amusement. The cavern they were in was so vast that the ceiling and the walls vanished from view into the shadows. Huge fires blazed, some on the ground, some high up on rocky protuberances. Figures scurried from one place to another, hurried on their way by the stinging end of a whip if they hesitated or seemed to deviate from their task. Great machines rumbled and roared, eating into the rock like voracious dinosaurs, as weary Creations ceaselessly stoked the fires, struggling to lift the heavy baskets of wood needed to keep them burning. Everywhere he looked was a straining hive of frantic activity.

Then came that blood-curdling wail again and Crevitos whipped the cart back to life, pushing it faster now as though there were something that he simply must not miss.

The cart lurched to a halt as the track ended. Crevitos leapt lithely out, beckoning impatiently for Saddler to follow.

The wailing rose in pitch and intensity, but Saddler was so horrified by what he saw that the noise faded momentarily into insignificance. All around them in this part of the cavern were enormous cauldrons, full of some noxious, viscous looking substance. It belched and spat like molten lava and the stench was so vile it made Saddler gag.

Crevitos hurried them to a small ledge where they would have a perfect view of the proceedings. He pointed to the nearest cauldron with barely contained excitement, but Saddler's gaze was already riveted to it with horrified fascination.

A Creation, not dissimilar in looks to a human being was being dragged screaming and struggling to the cauldron. The guards holding it paused briefly to glance up at Crevitos. Crevitos gave them a nod of approval and the Creation was hoisted unceremoniously into the air. Its tormented scream was abruptly silenced as it was plunged into the heaving liquid and sank helplessly below the surface.

There was a brief moment when all the turmoil and noise seemed to ebb away. Saddler tried to turn away, but found he was rooted to the spot.

For the longest few seconds he had ever known, the contents of the cauldron stilled, the surface of the liquid as calm as a pond on a tranquil summer's day.

The next instant, all hell broke loose. The vile liquid churned. The Creation erupted from its depths, writhing and screaming, no longer just a human caricature, but a grotesque parody. Its body contorted with agony as the guards deftly scooped it out of the cauldron with a huge net.

Crevitos pulled at Saddler's sleeve and set off after the guards. Saddler followed numbly. Just a few yards away the guards disappeared through a steel door set into the rocky side of the cavern. Crevitos leapt lightly up some steps to one side and onto a platform, where he peered through an observation hole in the side of the rock. He motioned Saddler to do the same. Sickened, but unable to refuse, Saddler did as he was told.

What he saw was a kind of antechamber with a large vat in the centre. Even from this distance Saddler could see that whatever was in the vat was so cold that a thin layer of ice had formed across the top. Blanching at the thought, Saddler had no doubts what was coming next.

He found the strength to turn away, but was unable to blot out the horrendous shrieks of shock and pain as the traumatized creature was lowered bit by bit into the vat.

'Slowly does it,' murmured Crevitos, 'we don't want you to fracture, my lovely!'

Saddler could not believe what he was hearing. He stared across the hellish scene to where the cart sat empty and waiting. Could he make it across without being caught? And if he did, what then?

But Crevitos had other ideas.

'Look!' he commanded. He grabbed Saddler's collar, virtually lifting him off the ground, so that he faced the antechamber one more. Miserably Saddler looked and, as he did so, the horrendous wail that he had heard before began to reverberate around the chamber. The wretched creature now crouched on a plinth that had risen up in the centre of the vat. As Saddler watched, the viscous substance from the cauldron began to freeze, forming tight, brittle scales everywhere except the creature's throat, palms and feet.

Finally, after what could only have been a minute, but must have felt like a lifetime to the pitiful creature below, the process was complete.

At last the wailing stopped. Shackled and broken, the creature shuffled behind the guards, but not before raising its head to where Crevitos and Saddler stood watching.

Saddler recoiled.

There was simply nothing left behind those dull, lifeless eyes.

CHAPTER FORTY-FOUR

Saddler barely noticed the journey back up to Crevitos's tower, despite the pain in his back and legs from the long climb. In Crevitos's bleak chamber, he sat numbly on the bed. His mind was so traumatized by what he had just witnessed that, for the moment it refused to process the information. Crevitos had left the tower almost immediately after their return. Saddler had not noticed the thoughtful look on Crevitos's face, but had just been glad to be left alone.

At some point, unaware of his own actions, Saddler had lain down on the bed. He drifted in and out of sleep, troubled by those same images he had seen the first time he was brought up to the tower. In one of his waking moments it occurred to him vaguely that he must have been in the mines before. Maybe that was where the gateway had taken him.

He was briefly conscious of Crevitos's return, but had no sense of how much time had passed. The next thing he knew for certain was the warm, bitter taste of the herbal concoction sliding between his lips and down his throat. Much as his brain would have preferred a continued oblivion, his body was now revitalized. Saddler had no option but to wake up and start the process of coming to terms with a procedure he could barely comprehend.

At length he sat up on the edge of the bed, only to find that Crevitos was sitting in the desk chair quietly watching him. Crevitos's expression was again thoughtful. He seemed calm, but energy radiated from him like a magnetic force.

There was a knock at the door. When Crevitos opened it, Saddler shrank back in horror, memories of what he had witnessed flooding back like a tidal wave. A creature entered carrying a large tray. Obviously Crevitos had ordered refreshments, but Saddler barely noticed. His eyes were riveted to the creature.

There was no doubt in his mind where he'd seen it before; the dull copper coloured scales, the dead eyes – was this the very same creature or just one of many?

The creature dully placed the tray on Crevitos's desk. As it turned to go, Saddler couldn't restrain a gasp from escaping his lips. A long, thin rat-like tail hung from its waist, looped and was fastened by a belt at its side.

Then the creature was gone and Saddler stared uncomprehendingly at Crevitos. Crevitos's lip curled. He was enjoying this. Then his face took on a serious expression.

'We have much to discuss,' he said, 'but first we eat.'

The last thing Saddler felt like doing was eating, but it crossed his mind that if there were to be any chance of him escaping at all, he would need to keep his energy levels up. Reluctantly he accepted what Crevitos offered. There was a kind of flat bread and cheese and some type of fruit he had not come across before, which had hints of apple, strawberry and coconut about it.

The food was delicious and Saddler realized he had no idea how long it was since he'd last eaten. His unexpected hunger brought with it pangs of guilt. His mind chose this moment to bring Anthony, Destiny and Boff to the fore and his stomach lurched as he pictured their concern when he didn't return.

What an idiot, he berated himself. You've only gone and ruined everything!

At last the repast was finished. Crevitos brushed a couple of imaginary crumbs from his front and leant forwards, resting his elbows on his knees. He pinned Saddler to attention with his gaze.

'There are many things to talk about and then I have a proposition for you!'

Saddler couldn't even begin to imagine what kind of 'proposition' Crevitos might want to put to him. Not to mention it was probably highly unlikely that any proposition suggested by Crevitos would have a refusal option attached.

Crevitos pulled his chair forward so that his knees were virtually touching Saddler's. It was uncomfortably close. Saddler had to force himself to stay where he was and resist the urge to shift further back on the bed.

Crevitos's eyes were burning with a passion so intense that Saddler could almost feel its scorching heat. Suddenly Crevitos leapt up; he appeared unable to contain the energy that coursed through him.

'Power!' he exclaimed as he paced the floor, 'is really all that matters. Knowing what you want and having the power to make it happen.'

He spun to face Saddler. 'I want...everything! I want to be the ultimate ruler of every world it is possible to reach. What you have witnessed is just the beginning, but soon, very soon I will have created the most powerful army the Cosmos has ever seen!'

Crevitos sat back down and peered intently at Saddler through narrowed eyes.

'And you are going to help me!'

There was tense silence, while Saddler tried to digest this unpalatable piece of information. Then Crevitos was on his feet again, pacing like a caged wild animal.

'My army will be invincible. Already it is strong, very strong. You were impressed, were you not by my fighting Creation!' It was spoken as a command rather than a question, but Saddler's revulsion at what he'd seen prompted him to retort, 'If you mean that poor creature I saw your bullies torturing...'

Crevitos laughed loudly.

'No pain, no gain! I admit the procedure is clumsy and lengthy, but it is remarkably effective. Not only are my Creations virtually indestructible, their minds become totally malleable to my will!'

Crevitos turned to his desk and snatched up some papers, which he thrust into Saddler's hands. There were a number of drawings of Creations of varied types. Saddler looked at Crevitos bewildered. Crevitos snatched the papers back impatiently. He waved them feverishly in the air.

'These are the very essence of my army. Each one of my fighting Creations has, as you've witnessed, body armour of the like never seen before. It has taken my scientists years of experimentation and failure and, just as I was close to despair we discovered a substance tougher, more resilient and more powerful than anything we had come across before...'

'Diamond,' whispered Saddler, as understanding dawned. He was fascinated, despite everything.

'Just so,' smiled Crevitos. 'All the years of fruitless experimenting at last repaid. We had the missing ingredient. The one thing that could be used to create an impenetrable armour. But still...' Crevitos face creased into a frown, '...still there are drawbacks. A huge amount of powdered diamond is needed for each single amount of substance, which means that hundreds of Creations who could be adapted are needed for digging in the mines.'

'That creature you manufactured,' said Saddler disgusted, 'was totally dead behind the eyes. It might be totally invincible, but I don't understand 'ow it suddenly becomes an aggressive fighting machine!'

Crevitos threw his head back. 'Suddenly,' he roared, 'is exactly the point! There is no suddenly. Each one has to be totally retrained. True, they have no will to be uncooperative or disobedient, but time is of the essence. My scientists are on the very cusp of discovering how to enlarge the size of the gateways into other worlds. Once we can open a large enough pathway to let through an army, I want to be ready to strike whilst we still have the element of surprise!'

Saddler had a sinking feeling he already knew the answer to his next question, but he still felt compelled to ask it.

'Where in particular are you in such a 'urry to conquer?'

Crevitos's generous-sized mouth stretched widely into an

appreciative grin. He knew exactly what Saddler was asking and this was a moment to savour.

'I think we both know the answer to that,' he said smoothly.

'What has Emajen done to deserve such a doubtful privilege?' groaned Saddler.

Crevitos breathed in deeply and exhaled slowly. He licked his lips as though anticipating some delicate morsel.

'Emajen,' he said slowly, 'is by far the strongest and most powerful world we have discovered so far.'

He paused.

Saddler waited.

Crevitos continued, 'Emajen has two things no other place that we have encountered does. It has mind power, and it has the Natorqua. The Natorqua, as you know are being dealt with. Without their steadying influence, everything will fall into disarray and once that happens, a lack of collective mind power will render it very weak and ineffective.'

Saddler attempted to leap from the bed. He wanted to pound Crevitos and wipe the sardonic smile off his face. But his strength had not yet fully returned and his knees buckled, forcing him to flop back down on the bed once again.

Crevitos was unfazed. 'Your world's mind power is an interesting concept,' he continued. 'I do hope your friends didn't begrudge me my little bit of fun!' He smirked.

Then his expression hardened. 'But now the time for fun is over. I have you here and without you I doubt your little friends will cause me any more bother!'

'I wouldn't underestimate 'em,' muttered Saddler, but his words were lost on Crevitos for whom, at least for the time being Destiny, Anthony and Boff had now ceased to exist.

Perched on his chair once more, Crevitos commanded Saddler's attention with his mere physical proximity.

'Recently, I visited a world called Earth, a place I believe you know rather well. There was something…someone I needed to see.'

For just a fraction of a second, Crevitos sounded less sure of himself.

Saddler was instantly alert. Was this a chink in Crevitos's armour? His Achilles heel?

Crevitos recovered himself almost immediately however.

'People on Earth are not so greatly different to those on Emajen, as I've no doubt you're aware. They have the same capacity to use the power of their minds, but they've grown dull and lazy.' Crevitos paused and then smiled. 'I see you are familiar with what I'm talking about. It seems that many of them still have power behind their thoughts but are totally unaware of it!

'Do you know how Creations come into existence?' he asked abruptly.

Saddler nodded.

'Then you will also know that it is exactly that strength of mind power, possessed by these people on Earth that gives Creations substance – some more so than others.'

Saddler nodded again.

'I have watched you closely,' mused Crevitos. 'A weaker mortal would have crumbled in the face of such adversity. But you are strong – very strong!'

Crevitos leant forward until Saddler was almost breathing the same breath.

'My army will be limitless. I can design Creations that are very nearly indestructible, but they all have a weakness – a part where the protective armour simply will not cling. And beneath the armour they are nothing, mere shadows easily dispatched.'

Crevitos rose from the chair and started pacing again, clearly agitated.

'My strength will grow with every conquest I make – but in the meantime, every Creation I draw saps my energy.'

'Why is that? Because you're 'aving to draw so many?'

'No, no!' Crevitos was impatient and wound up tightly like a coiled spring. 'My creator lost interest before I had the chance to draw enough strength from him. A few more weeks were all I needed...'

Saddler sat up abruptly.

Crevitos was a Creation!

He was the evil figment of some human being's imagination. Had he gone to Earth to see if he could find his creator? To see if somehow he could siphon the energy from him he so badly needed? It seemed that he had failed, but had he now found a way to make up for it?

'So what is it you think that I can do for you, Crevitos?' he asked quietly.

Crevitos stopped pacing abruptly.

'You are not a Creation and I am greatly impressed by your inner strength. I want you to draw my fighting Creations for me! With your vital force in their veins, they would be strong and robust and we could eliminate their weaknesses completely!'

'You're forgetting one thing.'

Crevitos raised an eyebrow enquiringly.

'Why on Emajen should I agree to help you?'

'It's something I've given much thought to. I will of course need a second in command; one with brains that is. Once conquered, Emajen could be yours to do with as you wish – after all, with so many worlds to conquer, I can't be everywhere at once.' Crevitos's expression took on a sly twist as he looked intently at Saddler. 'And if that isn't quite tempting enough, there are always your little friends to consider. I assume you would like them to be able to return to Earth...'

Saddler didn't need any further clarification to understand exactly what Crevitos meant.

'Sounds like an offer I could hardly refuse!' he said dryly.

Crevitos grinned. 'There is a slight catch,' he said.

'When isn't there,' said poor Saddler.

'I can't risk any...shall we say...uncertainty on your part marring the perfection of my fighting Creations. If you agree to help me, it will mean drinking a potion to eradicate your memory. Your mind will be a bright, blank page ready and willing to do my bidding.'

'So how do I know you'll keep to your end of the bargain?'

'Because I have said it will be so!' Crevitos actually looked genuinely offended.

From nowhere the seed of a plan planted itself in Saddler's mind: a very small seed, but better than nothing. If it didn't work, all was lost anyway. And really, he had no choice.

Saddler stayed silent for a few moments as though considering Crevitos's offer. His heart began to thump uncomfortably loudly and he was certain that Crevitos would hear it and know something was afoot. Taking a deep breath in an effort to calm his voice, he finally said, 'If I agree, when will this 'appen?'

Crevitos let out a roar of victorious laughter.

'No time like the present!' he crowed. He held out a small phial, much like the one Saddler had supped from before. He undid the stopper and held it out to Saddler.

Saddler raised the phial to his lips.

With one, last desperate glance at Crevitos, he closed his eyes and felt the cool, sweetish liquid slide over his tongue. As his throat muscles automatically contracted in a swallow, he slipped his free hand into his pocket.

Then Saddler was no more!

CHAPTER FORTY-FIVE

A cold, restless and dismal night was followed by an equally chill and cheerless dawn. Anthony, Destiny and Boff ate a meagre breakfast in morose silence. A light, dreary drizzle did nothing to lift their spirits.

At length Anthony shook himself out of his reverie and stood up, shaking crumbs from his jeans. Rummaging in his rucksack, he ferreted out the egg timer and peered at it intently.

'This isn't good,' he said.

Destiny and Boff looked up at him and gazed dismally at the egg timer, which now had barely a fifth of the sand remaining at the top.

'We can't wait here!' Anthony said firmly. 'Something's happened to Saddler or he would have been back by now!'

'But what can we do?' asked Destiny. 'We don't know where we are, let alone where we're going and supposing he does come back and finds out we've gone on without him?'

'Look at the timer! It's no good! Without Saddler and without the map, we've only got one option – we'll have to try and retrace our steps.'

'Um...' Boff's light bulbs started glowing a rosy pink colour. 'I have the map. Saddler had too much in his rucksack!'

Destiny flung her arms around Boff and squeezed him until his bulbs flashed alarmingly. Anthony laughed, and all at once, the stress of the situation eased. Destiny planted a kiss on Boff's cheek.

'You're a star!' She beamed.

Carefully stowing the timer back in his rucksack, Anthony sat back down again and took the map from Boff. The other two peered at it over his shoulder.

'Here's the old town we were at,' said Anthony, pointing to its position on the map, 'so I figure we must be somewhere around...here. Saddler reckoned he could reach the new town and back in about three hours – look, he's marked it here. It would have taken us slightly off our route, because the last place the Natorqua were seen is here.'

Boff's bulbs flashed briefly. 'So by that reckoning, if we follow the straightest route from here, it shouldn't take us more than a day to reach them!'

'As long as we don't have any more delays, then yes,' said Anthony.

'Saddler wouldn't want us to give up now,' said Destiny. 'Whatever's happened to him I vote we should carry on!'

'We don't have the faintest idea what we're supposed to do when we get there,' cautioned Anthony.

'Neither did Saddler, but he trusted us to help him,' said Destiny.

'There's a good chance we'll run out of time – I dread to think what our parents will do when they find out we're missing!'

'Well there's no guarantee we'll get back in time anyway. And what if Crevitos succeeds in doing here what he did to Doodland...' Destiny leapt to her feet in agitation. 'Anthony, we can't just let Emajen die! We've got to at least try...'

Anthony grinned. 'That's settled then. I just wanted you to be sure! Boff?'

Boff stood and hitched up his tartan shorts.

'What are we waiting for?' he said.

Not long after the sun had reached its peak, the trees began to thin and the vista became one of high, rolling hills. Consulting the map once more, they could see that there was a broad valley beyond the hills and, according to the cross marked on the map, it was where the Natorqua were last seen.

They all agreed that they would stop for a brief rest. If they could at least reach the valley before dark then maybe they would find the Natorqua the following day.

Despite the constant drizzling rain, they were heartened by

the hope that they were at least nearing their goal.

From a distance, the hills looked smooth and green and easy to climb, but the reality was vastly different. The first hill they climbed was pitted with awkward holes and crevices, hidden by innocent looking tufts of tangled grass and fern that caved in beneath the lightest tread.

Boff was the first to discover this. With a yell, he disappeared from view, arms flailing, bulbs sparking in terror. Fortunately, the hole he chose to vanish into was roughly a Boff-sized one. Apart from being shaken and somewhat dusty, he was unharmed, but Anthony's face was grim.

'There's no telling how deep some of these holes might be – we'll have to be extra careful!'

Their slow progress was made even slower by this realisation and it was well into the afternoon by the time they reached the top of the first hill. The sight that greeted them at the summit however was far from cheering; yet another stretch of hills that rose higher than the one they had just climbed.

Destiny flumped down in despair. 'We'll never get there,' she groaned.

The others flopped down beside her, but Anthony knew it would be fatal to stop for long. After a couple of minutes he got up and dragged Destiny to her feet.

'Look,' he said, 'even though the next hill is higher, it actually begins about two thirds of the way down this one, so we haven't really got all that far to climb.'

It was true. The hill they were on ended in a kind of dip part of the way down and then rose up again, just like the humps of some giant prehistoric serpent.

They slithered cautiously down the slope, which, on this side, didn't seem to be so covered in knotted ferns and so it was much easier to avoid any cracks. They stopped again for a few moments at the bottom of the second hill.

'I think we should empty our bags of anything we don't

absolutely need,' suggested Anthony. 'I doubt very much whether we'll have time to be making tea once we find the Natorqua!'

Boff was reluctant to leave their belongings behind, but Anthony assured him that they would stash them safely and mark the spot for when they returned.

'You're surely not leaving the timer?' Boff was aghast when he saw Anthony placing it with the things to be left behind.

'It's too late to worry about it now, Boff. It'll still be here when we get back!'

'And if we don't come back?' asked Destiny quietly.

'Then I guess we won't be needing it anyway!'

The shadows were just beginning to lengthen as they started to climb once more. Although there were far fewer crevices to watch out for, the foliage was also sparser and as they scrambled upwards, their feet slipped constantly – sending showers of loose debris bouncing and rattling down the hillside below them.

At one point they stopped on a convenient ledge to rest. Destiny looked down at how little ground they seemed to have covered and her heart sank. The sun was definitely beginning to dip now and there was a chill nip in the air.

'We need to get moving,' said Anthony anxiously. 'If we don't make it to the top before dark then we need to at least find somewhere more sheltered we can stop for the night!'

The others nodded in weary agreement and heaved themselves to their feet. Thankfully, the ground seemed to become more stable the higher they climbed, which helped them to make better progress. Here and there, tantalising niches appeared in the hill face, but none were big enough to shelter in. As the shadows deepened, Anthony became increasingly anxious about being stranded, unprotected on the hillside.

They passed a ledge that might reasonably accommodate the three of them and he was just about to suggest stopping there, when Boff gave a shout. He had lagged behind a little and was now gesticulating feverishly, a little to the left and higher up than the ledge. Anthony followed the direction of Boff's gaze and his face broke into a wide grin.

'You're a genius, Boff!' he yelled as he started to pick his way carefully through the dusk towards the mouth of a small fissure. A couple of minutes later, Destiny and Boff both appeared in the entrance, slightly out of breath. It was a very cramped space, but it would do.

Allowing themselves one biscuit each from their seriously depleted food supply, they all made themselves as comfortable as possible. Boff had insisted that they bring the orb and they were grateful now for its gentle glow, dispelling the chill of the night.

'This reminds me of the last time we slept in a cave,' said Destiny. 'I'm so glad we met you, Boff, but I hope there aren't any hidden entrances at the back of this cave!'

'I had a good look,' said Anthony, 'but there's hardly room to breathe let alone fit a secret entrance.'

'I hope Saddler's all right,' murmured Destiny, as her eyes closed.

'He's probably raising an army as we speak!' said Anthony, and he stared into the darkness willing it to be true.

Before long, they had all succumbed to an exhausted sleep and nothing occurred that night to trouble or disturb their slumber.

As a grey dawn filtered through the cave entrance, Anthony opened his eyes and stretched. It took him a few moments to recall where he was and to realize that this wasn't part of some complicated dream. Beside him, Boff and Destiny both stirred, rubbing their eyes and massaging stiff joints in a disturbingly similar manner.

It was still early, not yet entirely light. Wordlessly, Boff handed each a biscuit and a mere two minutes later they were ready for the last leg of their hill climb.

The day was strange. The sun rose in a cloudless sky and yet, as it climbed it seemed to spread very little light or warmth. What would normally have been a perfect, golden autumn day was somehow just dull and still; the only sounds were those they made scrambling up the craggy hill.

Anthony was the first to reach the summit. He stood, motionless, waiting for the others to join him.

What they saw when they reached the top took their breath away. Below them stretched a wide valley, through which ran a clear stream. It sparkled even in the plain, dull light. The bottom of the hill gave way to a dense wood of proud, ancient trees laden with fruit every colour of the rainbow. Beyond the stream, lay a vast lush meadow, carpeted in creamy yellow buttermilk flowers that Anthony immediately recognized from his dream.

And in the meadow, graceful and sleek, grazed the magnificent Natorqua.

CHAPTER FORTY-SIX

Destiny sat down hard, as though her legs simply couldn't support her weight.

'Oh!' was all she could utter.

Anthony and Boff sat down beside her. For a while it was all they could do just to sit and gaze in awe and wonder at the scene before them.

At last, Destiny sighed. 'They look so peaceful. Could Saddler have been wrong about them after all?'

'Well, we can't sit here all day,' said Boff matter-of-factly. 'We've come this far, it's about time we took a closer look.'

They scrambled and slid down the hillside, their hopes raised by the sight of the Natorqua grazing peacefully below.

If it weren't for the strange metallic murkiness of the light around them, it could well have seemed that all was right with the world.

At the bottom of the hill they found a rough stony path that led away, through the trees in the direction of the stream. Boff was looking rather hot and flustered, so Destiny relieved him of the one remaining backpack, which she flung lightly over one shoulder. They set off along the path, feeling much more positive now that they had nearly reached their goal.

The pathway meandered among the trees, sometimes allowing them a brief glimpse of the stream and sometimes almost seeming to curve back on itself so that they lost sight of the stream altogether. At one point, the stream was so close that Boff gave a whoop of joy and bounded off the path towards it. Anthony and Destiny watched aghast as he vanished totally from sight.

For what seemed like an age, they shouted his name until they were both hoarse, but of Boff there was no further sign.

In grim silence, they set off once more, keeping strictly to the middle of the path; not daring to risk the slightest stumble that might cause them to set a foot on the ground beyond.

Without warning they stepped out of the trees and there was the stream, glinting and burbling no more than a stone's throw away. The path ended where a small wooden bridge spanned the width of the stream.

'We made it!' said Anthony softly.

'I wish I knew if Boff was all right! First Saddler and now him!'

I don't like the look of that sky,' said Anthony, ruefully eyeing several purple bruises on the horizon.

Destiny slid the rucksack off her shoulder and flung it on the ground. She sank wearily on to a nearby boulder.

'What do we do now?'

Anthony squatted down beside her. He picked up a handful of stones from the path and weighed them absently in his hand.

Destiny gasped. 'Nebiré!' she said breathlessly. 'The vision in the crystals – this was it, remember! She said we would know what to do!'

'So she did – what did I do? Yes, I remember!'

Anthony scooped some of the stones from the path into a pile. He spread them out with a swift movement, watching as they settled, a couple rolling a little away from the main group and one or two trembling until they were finally still.

'Well?' asked Destiny.

'I don't know – it doesn't seem to mean anything!' Anthony peered worriedly at the stones again and shook his head. They both sat in silence for a few minutes, looking perplexedly at the pattern before them.

At that moment, a single ray of sun broke through the thick, purple-grey clouds and shone for a brief second on just one stone in the centre of the pattern. The stone shimmered for a fleeting moment with a pearly, rainbow-coloured luminescence. Then the ray was gone. Destiny looked at Anthony.

'That stone must be the key,' she said.

'I think you're right. Let's hope we can work out how!' agreed Anthony. He scooped the stone up and put it in his pocket.

'Right, I think we'd better see what kind of reaction we get from the Natorqua!' he said.

CHAPTER FORTY-SEVEN

The Natorqua continued to graze contentedly, as Anthony and Destiny made their way across the rickety wooden bridge. The herd was widely dispersed over the meadow and most were at some distance from the children; even so, Destiny set the rucksack down carefully, afraid that any sudden movement might cause a panic amongst the herd.

In quiet undertones, they agreed that Anthony should try to approach the nearest Natorqua on his own. Destiny watched as he moved slowly and calmly through the calf-high flowers towards the nearest animal. When he was no more than a few yards away, the Natorqua raised its head and looked directly at him. Anthony lowered his gaze to show that he wasn't posing a threat and continued his unhurried approach.

The Natorqua had dropped its head to continue grazing, but with Anthony's very next step its head snapped up again, sharply.

Everything happened with unimaginable speed. Anthony's mind was blasted with several things, all in one split second. His ears detected Destiny's cry of warning at the very same fraction of an instant that the beautiful, serene creature before him snarled furiously, eyes flashing, and razor sharp canines bared in menace. In this same moment, Anthony's mind was consumed by a scarlet furnace of hatred and rage that rooted him like a steel spike to the spot on which he stood.

He had no time to react.

The Natorqua reared, spun and charged.

The last thing Anthony heard was Destiny's high-pitched scream, before the world began to revolve and then ceased to be.

* * *

'Anthony? Anthony? Are you okay?'

The voice sounded familiar, but in his confused state, Anthony couldn't quite place it. He opened his eyes cautiously, not entirely sure where he was or how he happened to be here.

Several faces were peering down at him, Destiny...and... and someone... He closed his eyes for a moment, willing the muzziness in his head to dissipate. Then his eyes sprang open again.

'Boff? Squib? Prof?'

Boff's triangle mouth grinned down at him and Destiny's worried frown uncreased as she too broke into a relieved smile.

'Thank goodness, I thought maybe you were...you know...'

'No chance,' Anthony groaned as he raised himself circumspectly into a sitting position. 'You can't get rid of me that easily! Where are we anyway? And where did you *get* to Boff?'

'Well, it was a very strange thing!' said Boff.

It would seem that as Boff had stepped off the path everything simply disappeared into a white fog. He had called frantically and tried to step back the way he had come, but whichever direction he turned in, the result was the same – pure, white nothing. Nor did his other senses help him in any way; there was nothing to see and equally nothing to hear, smell or feel. It was as though he had stepped into a complete void.

For a while he had sat cross-legged on the ground, wondering if perhaps whatever it was might clear. He had absolutely no way of knowing how much time had passed, though it seemed as though it must be an age, when he heard a voice calling.

'Boff! Hey, Boff! Are you all right? He's not responding Squib... Speak to me, Boff! Where are the others? Where are Destiny and Anthony? Oh, Poor Boff, what on Emajen has happened to you?'

All these questions took Boff quite by surprise. The voice sounded familiar and it was very close, but he could still see nothing. Then it occurred to him abruptly; hadn't the voice mentioned Squib? Confused and bewildered, he was just about to open his mouth and call out, when something gently touched his shoulder. Two things had then happened simultaneously: Boff jumped violently and the white fog disappeared.

There he was sitting on the forest floor no more than a stone's throw from the path and standing in front of him, with concerned expressions on their faces, were the Prof and Squib.

'What?'

Poor Boff just couldn't fathom what was happening. The Prof knelt down in front of him.

'Are you okay, Boff?'

'Yes, I think so. What happened to the fog?'

'We didn't see any fog, just you sitting on the ground looking lost. It seems that somebody or something is still playing mind games. So where are Destiny and Anthony?'

Boff had just started to explain when a shrill cry reached them from somewhere across the stream.

'Destiny,' yelled Boff.

Before he and the Prof had gained their feet, Squib was gone. With the speed of forked lightning, he disappeared in the direction of the scream, leaving the others to follow as swiftly as they could.

Anthony rubbed at his temples, trying to take in the full import of this story and aware of the dull ache that seemed to throb almost constantly behind his eyes.

'So how did you come to be in the woods,' he asked the Prof.

'Ah, well, I can take no credit for that at all. Young Squib here saw these rather interesting storm clouds gathering and insisted that we follow in your footsteps to see if there was anything we could do to help. He's a very intuitive soul; I more than trust his instincts.' Here the Prof shook his head, 'Sadly, from what Destiny says, we were too late to help Saddler!'

Anthony's face clouded. 'We don't even know if he's still alive.'

He looked around. They seemed to be in some kind of small wooden dwelling. He had been laid on a hard bed. There was a table and chairs, a rough fireplace and a wooden chest in one corner, but the place looked and felt as though it had been deserted for a long time. Anthony rubbed his head again.

'You said you heard a cry! I don't remember that – I don't remember it at all. What happened?'

'I can't believe you don't remember anything!' Destiny was aghast.

'I think, yes, we were standing over there in the meadow and I was walking to the Natorqua – but after that it's all just a blank!'

Destiny shook her head and began to tell him what had happened; how everything had seemed calm and serene and fine until suddenly, without warning the Natorqua had turned into a raging demon.

'I thought...I don't know...that you would be crushed. It turned on you so fast!' Destiny's face turned a ghastly white as the memory of that moment came back to her with full force. Tears began to trickle down her cheeks as the shock of what had happened and what so easily might have happened finally hit home. She wiped them away furiously and continued, albeit with a slight wobble in her voice.

'It launched itself at you – I can't think of any other way to describe it! It looked like it wanted to pound you into the ground. But you didn't move; you just seemed to be rooted to the spot. And I thought, I thought it would trample you or bite your head off or something and I yelled at you to move, but you didn't and then – then there was Squib, tearing across the field.

'He was so brave. He stood over you, right underneath those awful, thrashing hooves and then, I think he started throwing something...'

'Stones,' said Squib.

'Yes, stones. He just kept hurling them and for whatever reason, it just seemed to wake the Natorqua up out of its rage and the next thing, the whole herd was thundering away across the meadow.'

Destiny ran out of puff. She looked helplessly at Anthony. From out of nowhere, a flash of raw, red anger suffused his mind, making him shudder. His forehead knitted into a frown as he desperately tried to remember. The throbbing ache had now spread around his whole head in a tight, oppressive band. It increased in intensity until he thought his head might split in two. Then it was gone and he was left with a quiet sense of certainty.

He turned to Destiny and the others and smiled at them wearily.

'They'll be back,' he said.

'What then?' asked Boff.

'Then Destiny and I have a job to do, but for now I think we need to try and get some rest. I've a feeling we've all got a tough time ahead of us!'

Surprisingly, cramped and uncomfortable as the arrangements were, they all slept, although it was impossible to know how long for since the sky had barely changed colour, apart from the fact that the purple bruises seemed to have merged and spread and slightly darkened.

Anthony had awoken feeling barely refreshed. Disturbing dreams had tortured his sleep, which faded quickly now, but left him feeling ill at ease and certain that the answers he needed were all there if only he could reach them.

Boff was determined to keep everyone's spirits up. At least there was no need for them to starve. He set off with Squib to gather fruit from the trees and to fetch water from the stream.

Anthony and Destiny stood gazing out of the window. Sure enough, as Anthony had predicted, the Natorqua had returned. They looked as placid and serene as ever. Destiny could barely believe she had really witnessed such savage fury the day before.

Boff and Squib returned, laden with goodies. By some

incredible fluke (and Boff swore blind he had no idea how it could have possibly happened) the tea appeared to have been missed when it came to emptying out unnecessary items from the rucksack. Despite their sombre mood, Destiny awarded Boff a warm smile.

'You're a star,' she said.

While Destiny unearthed some rather dusty mugs and a teapot from the crate near the hearth, Anthony and the Prof managed to get a small fire going. For just a short space of time they all sat and enjoyed the sweet, refreshing taste of the crisp fruit and sipped gratefully at their hot mugs of tea.

Then Destiny sat back and looked at Anthony. He was leaning on the table, staring into space. It was the only time she thought she had ever seen him at a loss for what to do. He felt her gaze and looked up, giving her a wan smile.

'If only I could remember what happened! Tell me again.'

Destiny repeated the story, but Anthony just shook his head.

'I know it's there in my head – I had all those weird dreams to prove it, but it's all just out of reach!'

Suddenly, Destiny sat bolt upright. 'What about the stone!' Nebiré was right about the vision and she was positive we would know what to do!'

Slowly, Anthony reached into his pocket. He closed his hand around the stone, which felt curiously warm, almost hot to the touch. It pulsed beneath his fingers like a heartbeat and all at once he was back in the meadow, this time surrounded by the Natorqua. They circled him menacingly, lips curled, eyes rolling wildly.

He felt their fury. It suffocated him, stealing his breath. A scarlet mist obscured his vision and his cheeks were wet with tears. He tried to wipe the tears away, but when he looked down his hand dripped scarlet blood and still the tears continued to flow. He began to choke, his breath coming in ragged gasps.

The Natorqua had stopped circling and now stood facing

him, sapping his energy with their rage and anger like voracious vampires. The scarlet mist in front of his eyes began to darken to purple and then black.

He sank to his knees.

'Destiny,' he gasped. 'I can't...'

There was a searing flash that rent the sky from top to bottom. The Natorqua screamed. Rearing and thrashing they turned as one and thundered past Anthony, their fury transforming in an instant into mindless fear.

Only one remained. Lit by a lightning flash, it shone with a pearly luminescence – all the colours of the rainbow. It stared beseechingly at Anthony, eyes rolling with terror. Then it too was gone.

Anthony was left alone, but not for long.

Another searing flash lacerated the firmament, ripping a vast, black fissure through the very fabric of the sky. As he watched helplessly, the immense gash bulged like a vile, septic pustule waiting to erupt.

With a final heave, the colossal wound ruptured and a horde of foul, demonic creatures spewed forth from its festering depths.

Anthony gasped for breath, his lungs burning. He could hear voices screaming at him above the din. Without warning, his vision cleared and he lay, slumped across the table in the wooden cabin drenched with sweat. Boff was shaking him and Destiny was pleading with him from the window.

'Anthony, please, please wake up. We're too late. They're coming. It's too late!'

Trying desperately to shake off his vision, Anthony struggled to his feet and staggered to the window. He had no doubts as to what he would see there. The sky was now almost entirely a dark purple; the ground a heaving mass of black shapes, like a carpet of angry ants swarming over the meadow.

Streaks of forked lightning continued to ravish the sky, throwing stark flashes of brilliance onto the scene below.

Anthony dragged Destiny away from the window. He held her by the shoulders at arm's length.

'Look at me,' he yelled, barely able to hear himself. 'It's not too late. I know what we have to do!'

Destiny shook her head uncomprehendingly. 'What can we possibly do?' she mouthed, gesturing helplessly at the scene outside the window.

'We have to find the Alpha-female,' Anthony yelled.

There was an earth-shattering crash and the walls of the cabin began to shake. Anthony made a grab for Squib who was standing next to him and screamed, 'Get down!'

A violent splintering noise drowned out everything as the side of the cabin disintegrated around them.

The whole of the Natorqua herd stampeded through, obliterating everything in their path, scattering flying debris with their flailing hooves. As the last Natorqua galloped through the wreckage, Anthony hauled a gasping Destiny to her feet. The others scrambled from the ruins shaking dust and splinters from their hair and clothes.

'We have to follow them!' he said urgently, but before he could make off in the direction of the stampeding Natorqua, Destiny grabbed his arm.

'Look!' she said.

They all turned to see a figure on natorback galloping furiously across the meadow towards Crevitos's teaming army. Swarming behind him must have been virtually every inhabitant of Emajen, their frenzied cries echoing across the stream like a fanfare.

'Who?' They all looked at each other dumbstruck. It was Boff who pointed a shaking finger at the immense rip in the sky, where more and still more of Crevitos's fighting Creations poured through in a ceaseless flow of destruction.

Anthony grabbed Destiny's hand. 'We have to go. Now!'

He gestured to where the Natorqua were huddled in a

quivering group among the trees.

'Boff, Squib, will you stay here and keep watch – and keep us posted?'

They both nodded solemnly. Squib immediately made for the nearest tree and shinned up it nimbly.

Anthony gave him an appreciative thumbs up before turning to Destiny.

'If we can work out which one is the Alpha-female, we've got a chance. Crevitos has somehow twisted all their mind power to rage and aggression. The Alpha-female is the strongest. She knows something is wrong and has just about managed to keep the herd under control so far. But she won't be able to hold out for long. The stress and fury of the herd is wearing her down. Somehow we have to work with her, give her back her positive mind power. I can't do it on my own though, Destiny. These creatures are only half horse – that I can deal with. The cat half is your domain!'

'Well we'd better get started then!' said Destiny.

CHAPTER FORTY-EIGHT

Lightning slashed across the storm swept sky. Crevitos towered, deliberately menacing, as his dark cloak whipped around him, bullied by the brutish wind. He roared his pleasure as his black stallion reared and plunged beneath him.

Crevitos had been here before, in this scene of vicious, cruel domination. He could almost taste the victory. But this time it was better, far better than it had been in Doodland. There the Creations had crumbled before his wrath and cowered in humble supplication with barely a murmur of protest.

As he stood in the gateway between this world and his own, his steed now trembling with fear and excitement beneath him, Crevitos surveyed the approaching army with sadistic amusement. They didn't stand a chance against his supreme fighting force!

For just a brief moment, doubt flickered through his mind. Somehow Saddler had slipped through the net and Crevitos's army was not yet invincible, it was true. But what it lacked in strength was more than made up for in numbers; where these came from, there were many, many more to follow.

Crevitos raised his sword with a triumphant bellow and the power of his brutality swept like a tidal wave across his outlandish band of Creations. They answered with an echoing roar and surged towards their advancing enemy.

From where he perched in his tree, Squib watched with awe as the two great masses collided and clashed. The storm in the heavens continued to rage as furiously as the battle below, casting a ghoulish, flickering luminosity over the raging, seething mass of creatures. Rain had begun to fall silently, turning the churned and desecrated meadow into a slippery, sodden mud bath.

Boff watched mesmerized. At first the scene was nothing but a boiling, heaving mess of clashing bodies, but then a pattern seemed to emerge. Crevitos's army were falling like flies and the throng of Emajen's people would surge forward triumphantly. But then hordes more of Crevitos's Creations would pour through the rent in the sky and so the cycle would begin again.

Amongst the mayhem, Crevitos could be seen wheeling and turning and wielding his great sword. And there was the mysterious rider who had led the Emajen charge, feverishly spurring his followers on.

Suddenly there was a lull.

The two riders came face to face in the very core of the battle. The armies stopped fighting and there was a deathly hush.

Crevitos threw back his head and crowed with delight.

'You!' he spluttered, barely able to contain his glee.

'Yeah, me,' said Saddler quietly. 'Didn't quite work out 'ow you planned it, did it!'

Crevitos smirked and curled his lip scornfully. 'You, of all people, should know how vast my army is. They may not be invincible yet, but just how long do you think your puny little band of peasants can keep fighting without rest and sustenance? You don't have a hope!'

'Then we'll die trying!' said Saddler.

'Ha!' Crevitos's mirth reverberated like a shock wave across the meadow. 'And so you shall!' he cackled. He leant forward across his mount's sweating neck, his face no more than a hand's breadth from Saddler's. 'Watching you die will be an unforeseen pleasure!' he snarled.

With that he whipped his steed around and plunged back into the throng. As if a spell were broken the fighting began to rage once more in earnest.

'Saddler!' breathed Boff to himself. 'I would know that figure anywhere!'

Although he could hear none of the exchange that had taken place, it didn't take a genius to work out that Saddler's army were simply outnumbered. Squib had slipped unseen down from his perch. He and Boff consulted briefly and then melted quietly into the trees.

CHAPTER FORTY-NINE

The Natorqua had not moved for some considerable time. They simply stood together, heads hanging, eyes half closed as though completely drained of their will to live. Anthony and Destiny had crouched, watching desperately for a sign; the smallest flicker of a movement that would show them which Natorqua was the Alpha-female.

Then, to their horror, one of the Natorqua simply crumpled, its legs folding as it slid noiselessly to the ground.

'They're dying!' Destiny's voice was full of distress. 'We have to do something. We can't just sit here and watch them die!'

She looked at Anthony helplessly, but only saw her own anguish mirrored in his eyes.

There was a rustling sound behind them. Squib and Boff appeared through the trees. Boff's face was grim.

'Any luck?' he panted, trying to catch his breath.

'They're dying, Boff!' Destiny began to cry softly.

The Prof, who had been sitting quietly nearby, stood and put a comforting arm around her shoulders.

'You'll find a way, of that I'm certain!' Turning to Boff, he said, 'What's the news? How much time do we have?'

'Not good and not much I don't think,' Boff said gravely. 'There doesn't seem to be any end to Crevitos's supply of Creations. They fall, but more just keep coming. But we saw Saddler! He's the one leading Emajen's people!'

'Saddler!' exclaimed Anthony and Destiny at once.

'Don't ask me how, but he's here in the thick of it. He keeps rallying them all, but I don't know how much longer they can hold out.'

Destiny clutched her head in despair. 'What are we going to do?' she cried.

Anthony's mouth shot open. 'The *Stone*, why didn't I think of it sooner? It worked before…'

He reached into his pocket and drew out the stone. It lay still and dull and cold in his palm.

'I don't understand…' He looked at Destiny and then at the Prof, his expression a mixture of confusion and despair.

With a certainty that came from she knew not where, Destiny took Anthony's hand in hers. 'Nebiré said we have the mind power to reach all living things. We can do this!'

They stood quite still.

The world faded around them; all apart from the Natorqua huddled in their abject group just a few yards away.

They waited.

A single beam of sunlight lit up Destiny's face and Anthony felt the stone quiver to life in his hand. The stone shimmered and sparkled. A ray of pure, white light shot from the stone right into the very centre of the herd. The Alpha-female began to shimmer and sparkle too, reflecting every delicate colour of the rainbow.

Destiny felt the energy of the stone surge through Anthony's fingertips to hers and right through her whole being.

The Natorqua parted noiselessly as Destiny and Anthony approached the Alpha-female and stood completely still, watching.

The Alpha-female stood before them, majestic and beautiful, nostrils quivering. She pawed the ground once and was still. Slowly she lowered her sleek, feline head and allowed Anthony to stroke her soft, silky neck.

Anthony turned to Destiny and she was relieved to see a look of purpose on his face.

'She needs us to help her restore strength to the herd,' he said firmly.

He took Destiny's hands and placed them lightly on the Natorqua's neck.

'Close your eyes,' he said, placing his own hands over hers. 'Picture a time when you were at one with an animal. Focus on that time. Make it positive, so that she can draw power from you!'

Destiny closed her eyes and was immediately transported back in time to home and Torny playing with a silver ball on the end of a piece of string. But the string had somehow twisted itself around his paw. She saw the look of startled pain and fear in his bright round eyes. She saw her mother appear and cut the string and felt the soft, furry bullet that buried itself furiously in her arms, seeking reassurance and comfort. She realized in that moment how it was that she had known what to do for Harriet, the dog at the ranch. A feeling of pure joy radiated right through her and at the same time she felt tremendous power coursing through her hands from Anthony's.

The Alpha-female quivered.

There was an immense flash and a crack of thunder that shook the very ground beneath their feet and sent Anthony and Destiny sprawling.

The Alpha-female reared almost upright and they stared in awe as veins of lightning surged through her entire body. Her nostrils flared wide. She opened her mouth and a wild neigh of defiance split the air.

'Come on!' Anthony pulled Destiny to her feet and dragged her back towards the Natorqua. With a strength he didn't know he possessed, he hoisted Destiny up on to the Alpha-female's back and then sprang up lightly behind her. He looked around him for the others.

'Don't worry about us,' shouted the Prof. 'We'll follow.'

The Alpha-female pawed at the ground impatiently and they barely had time to cling on before she leapt into the air and galloped full pelt towards the meadow, the herd stampeding closely on her tail.

Saddler swung his axe with furious disgust at the lumbering creature before him. He aimed directly for its unprotected throat. The creature snarled, displaying razor sharp canines the size of large daggers and lunged at Saddler with nothing but a savage, gratuitous desire to kill behind its eyes.

With no qualm at all, Saddler landed his strike and the creature crumpled soundlessly beneath the blow. He watched the creature for a split second and then nodded grimly. How many Creations he had now killed was beyond count, but he felt no sense of guilt.

Saddler was by nature a gentle man and killing was not something he would do through choice, but his first blow in Doomland had been born out of sheer desperation: desperation to escape Doomland and desperation to save Emajen.

In the dark recesses of Crevitos's domain, Saddler had been forced to slay his first Creation – slay or be slain. He would have been of very little use to Emajen rotting away in some foul corner and so his momentary hesitation had been superseded by his need to live.

The creature had died easily showing no signs of pain or fear. Overcome with grief at his action, Saddler had watched the creature helplessly. In that instant, its face had softened and a look of peace had spread across its features. In that bizarre moment, Saddler had realized that he had in fact set its tortured soul free. From that point on, his survival and the subsequent battle had become a mercy mission on more than one level.

A brief lull allowed Saddler a moment to catch his breath. The fact that he knew all about the weaknesses of Crevitos's Creations had given Emajen's inhabitants a fighting chance to defend their world. Now though, it became all too obvious that Saddler's followers were beginning to flag. The sheer number of Creations that continued to pour through the rip between worlds gave them no chance of respite.

It occurred to him for the first time that they were going to lose. Emajen as he knew it was going to die and become a desolate clone of Doomland.

But he himself would die defending Emajen. With a piercing

shriek he plunged back into the fray.

A gigantic flash, more blinding than any that had come before, ripped the sky in two. The tremendous boom that followed shook the ground so hard that many were knocked clean off their feet. The ground continued to reverberate until an ominous pounding replaced the aftershock and the Natorqua came galloping into view; the whole herd illuminated by the vivid sparks of electricity that flashed among them.

With no hesitation, the Alpha-female carved through the battling bodies. The fighting stopped abruptly. All sounds of battle ceased. The Alpha-female slid to a halt directly in front of Crevitos. Anthony and Destiny quickly slipped down from her back.

The other Natorqua circled Crevitos while the Alpha-female stood proud and silent in front of him. The black stallion shifted uneasily. For a long time the Alpha-female and Crevitos tussled eye to eye. Neither moved.

'What are they doing?' hissed Destiny.

'Battle of wills!' breathed Anthony.

Then Crevitos threw his head back and snarled; his face contorted with fury. The Alpha-female roared. With magnificent power and beauty the whole herd reared as one. Fierce, multi-coloured flames erupted from their nostrils and at that very moment, Crevitos violently yanked his steed around.

Shards of flame sped across the sky, colliding with the enormous split that Crevitos now galloped towards. With each collision, the vast black tear shuddered and shrank. As it collapsed in on itself, Crevitos thundered ever closer, his stallion stumbling and foaming. Only yards away from the shrinking hole, Crevitos's mount collapsed beneath him; it quivered and was still. The Alpha-female gave one final roar and a bright gold flash of flame shot like an arrow from her nostrils across the sky. Crevitos stumbled towards the hole. He turned. His cry reverberated across the meadow and then he was gone, only a fraction of a second before the golden flame exploded where he had just stood.

The black tear imploded with a soft hiss and was gone.

There was a stunned silence and then Destiny felt something tug at her hand. It was Boff. 'Look!' he said, awe-struck.

All around the meadow, Crevitos's Creations crumpled and sank to the ground. As Emajen's inhabitants watched bemused, the expressions of violent fury melted from each Creation's face to be replaced by one of calm serenity.

Everyone looked at everyone else.

It began to dawn on them.

It was over.

With one accord, a triumphant cry of jubilation swept through the meadow and people were hugging each other and shedding tears of relief.

And in the midst of the celebrations, the Natorqua stood grazing tranquilly as though it were the most natural thing in the world.

Tentatively, Anthony and Destiny approached the Alpha-female, half afraid of breaking the spell of calm that surrounded the herd. As they drew near, she lifted her head and blew softly at them through her nostrils.

They exchanged looks. The power that emanated from the Alpha-female was exceptional and they felt it flow through their veins, suffusing them with strength and peace and a tremendous sense of well-being.

CHAPTER FIFTY

'Don't mean to spoil the moment, but I think it's 'igh time we got you two 'ome!'

A grin spread across Destiny's features and she flung herself at Saddler enveloping him in a hug that very nearly cut off his blood circulation.

Beaming from ear to ear, Saddler hugged Destiny back with one arm, whilst furiously pumping Anthony's hand up and down with the other.

'What *happened* to you?' gasped Destiny. 'We were so worried!'

Saddler's face clouded. 'It's a very long story and I *will* tell you one day, but now we 'ave to get you back before it's too late…if it isn't too late already!'

With a slightly shame-faced look, Boff produced the small egg timer from his shorts pocket.

Anthony grinned. 'What will we do without you?' he said.

Boff held the timer up high. Only two grains of sand remained in the top half and, as they watched, one of these slipped through the narrow middle and settled on the heap in the bottom.

'We're not going to make it, are we?' said Destiny. 'What happens if we don't?'

'I'd 'oped that maybe no one would notice you'd gone. But once your time restarts, several days could pass before we get you back there. I'm sorry. It's going to cause a lot of bother for you. We'd best get going!'

Just at that moment, Destiny felt a gentle shove in the small of her back. She turned to find the Alpha-female gazing at her softly. The Natorqua looked straight into Destiny's eyes and her meaning was clear.

'We've got a chance yet!' said Destiny excitedly.

Saddler lifted her and Boff onto the Alpha-female's back once more. Anthony sprang lightly on another.

'What about you?' Destiny asked.

'You're only light; you'll be quicker without me! You know where the box is – tell Mrs Saddler I'm fine and I'll be 'ome soon!'

Destiny's eyes filled with tears. 'Will we see you again?'

'Of cour...' But Saddler's answer was whipped away from her by the wind, as the Natorqua sprang forwards and sped swiftly across the meadow. They lightly leapt the stream and the countryside disappeared beneath them in a breath-taking blur.

The distance it had taken them so many days to travel was eaten up with careless ease. In no time at all, the familiar sight of Saddler's picturesque cottage swept into view. The two Natorqua glided smoothly to a standstill and the children and Boff slid to the ground.

Mrs Saddler appeared at the door to the cottage with a frying pan in her hand and a determined expression on her face. Seeing the children and Boff, she dropped the pan and flung her arms out wide. She bustled towards them exclaiming and questioning far too fast for them to give any response.

At last Anthony extracted himself from her relieved embrace for long enough to explain the bare bones of what had happened. He decided not to mention that Saddler had gone missing for a period of time. After all, they didn't know the full import of that story and it was enough for her to know that Saddler was all right and that he would soon return.

Mrs Saddler was rather over-awed by the Natorqua, but a gentle huff from the Alpha-female was enough to send her fussing to fetch water and apples and to have her exclaiming over their majesty and beauty.

Amazing, powerful creatures though they were, it wasn't lost on Anthony and Destiny that the Natorqua were just as susceptible to a bit of fuss and adoration as any animal back home.

Mindful that time was not on their side Anthony asked Mrs Saddler if they could have the box and the key. He explained about the egg timer, which Boff dutifully produced from his pocket. The last grain of sand chose that precise moment to slip quietly into the heap at the bottom. The timer glowed once and then disintegrated, the sand trickling away through Boff's fingers.

'Oh my word!' exclaimed Mrs Saddler. 'What was I thinking, chattering on? Your poor mother, she'll be 'orrified if she finds out you've gone!' She hurried off to fetch the box.

Destiny stroked the Natorqua gently.

'Thank you!' she said softly.

The Alpha-female rested her head lightly on Destiny's shoulder for a moment and a soft purr rumbled up from somewhere deep inside. Then, with a flick of their tails the Natorqua were gone.

Destiny turned to Boff who was shaking hands with Anthony. Her throat was too full for her to say anything. She just hugged him tight and gave him a watery smile.

Mrs Saddler appeared again with the box and key. Resting it carefully on the low wall, Anthony looked at the key in the palm of his hand.

'Isn't it about time you were going?' it said grumpily.

'At least some things don't change!' laughed Anthony. 'Take good care of Mrs Saddler until Saddler gets back, Boff!'

He placed the key in the lock and the bright light obliterated all around them, closely followed by the black inkblot. He grabbed Destiny by the hand and pulled her through.

Glancing back, the last thing Destiny saw was Boff's cheeky triangle grin as he called after her, 'Hey, Destiny, thanks for my tartan shorts!'

ACKNOWLEDGEMENTS

Writing these has to be almost as hard as writing the book itself; there are so many people along the way who offer help, guidance and support with such a project.

Firstly, a huge thank you to Professor Ian Parker, world renowned psychologist, editor and author but much more importantly (from my point of view) ever supportive big brother. Without him, Emajen simply wouldn't be published. My husband Tony deserves a medal for his unfailingly positive belief in my ability to write *Emajen* and to become a published author and for putting up with my terminal lack of self-assurance. Thank you also to my daughter Emma for her unwavering confidence in me. You are so much more street-wise than I will ever be. Thank you to my parents, M and Hugh for always supporting me through life's adventures this far. I hope I can finally make you proud. Thank you too, to my lovely sister Andrea for her endless patience and positive attitude and to brother-in-law Jamie for his superlative contract reading skills. My thanks must also go to Ian's partner, Professor Erica Burman, for being an inspiration to me and, I believe, women everywhere. To all my family and friends; thank you now and always for your unconditional love and support. Last, but by no means least, an immense thank you to John Hunt Publishing for giving me this opportunity and for all their help and support along the way. Invariably, acknowledgements end up as a list, whether you write them vertically or horizontally, which gives a false impression that some people are more important than others. The list can't be avoided; however, I am grateful in equal measure to everyone who has lent their support in any way.

OUR STREET
BOOKS

JUVENILE FICTION, NON-FICTION, PARENTING

Our Street Books are for children of all ages, delivering a potent
mix of fantastic, rip-roaring adventure and fantasy stories to excite
the imagination; spiritual fiction to help the mind and the heart;
humorous stories to make the funny bone grow; historical tales to
evolve interest; and all manner of subjects that stretch
imagination, grab attention, inform, inspire and keep the pages
turning. Our subjects include Non-fiction and Fiction, Fantasy and
Science Fiction, Religious, Spiritual, Historical, Adventure, Social
Issues, Humour, Folk Tales and more.
If you have enjoyed this book, why not tell other readers by
posting a review on your preferred book site. Recent bestsellers
from Our Street Books are:

Relax Kids: Aladdin's Magic Carpet
Marneta Viegas
Let Snow White, the Wizard of Oz and other fairytale characters
show you and your child how to meditate and relax. Meditations
for young children aged 5 and up.
Paperback: 978-1-78279-869-9 Hardcover: 978-1-90381-666-0

Wonderful Earth
An interactive book for hours of fun learning
Mick Inkpen, Nick Butterworth
An interactive Creation story: Lift the flap, turn the wheel, look in
the mirror, and more.
Hardcover: 978-1-84694-314-0

Boring Bible: Super Son Series 1
Andy Robb
Find out about angels, sin and the Super Son of God.
Paperback: 978-1-84694-386-7

Jonah and the Last Great Dragon
Legend of the Heart Eaters
M.E. Holley
When legendary creatures invade our world, only dragon-fire can
destroy them; and Jonah alone can control the Great Dragon.
Paperback: 978-1-78099-541-0 ebook: 978-1-78099-542-7

Little Prayers Series: Classic Children's Prayers
Alan and Linda Parry
Traditional prayers told by your child's favourite creatures.
Hardcover: 978-1-84694-449-9

Magnificent Me, Magnificent You The Grand Canyon
Dawattie Basdeo, Angela Cutler
A treasure filled story of discovery with a range of inspiring fun
exercises, activities, songs and games for children aged 6 to 11.
Paperback: 978-1-78279-819-4

Q is for Question
An ABC of Philosophy
Tiffany Poirier
An illustrated non-fiction philosophy book to help children aged
8 to 11 discover, debate and articulate thought-provoking, open-
ended questions about existence, free will and happiness.
Hardcover: 978-1-84694-183-2

Relax Kids: How to be Happy
52 positive activities for children
Marneta Viegas
Fun activities to bring the family together.
Paperback: 978-1-78279-162-1

Rise of the Shadow Stealers
The Firebird Chronicles
Daniel Ingram-Brown
Memories are going missing. Can Fletcher and Scoop unearth
their own lost history and save the Storyteller's treasure from the
shadows?
Paperback: 978-1-78099-694-3 ebook: 978-1-78099-693-6

Readers of ebooks can buy or view any of these bestsellers by clicking on the live link in the title. Most titles are published in paperback and as an ebook. Paperbacks are available in traditional bookshops. Both print and ebook formats are available online.

Find more titles and sign up to our readers' newsletter at
http://www.johnhuntpublishing.com/children-and-young-adult
Follow us on Facebook at https://www.facebook.com/JHPChildren
and Twitter at https://twitter.com/JHPChildren